"What Are You Frightened Of, O'Hara?"

Rafe asked softly.

Valentina bristled and reddened. "Frightened? I'm not. Why would I be?"

"Do I frighten you? After you slept in my arms for most of two nights, are you suddenly afraid that I would harm you?"

Shaking her head and catching the sweep of her hair back, she stuttered a denial. "I never…I wouldn't…"

"You dreamed, O'Hara," Rafe said, wishing he could touch her and comfort her as before. "Disturbing dreams. And I held you until you slept at peace."

Dear Reader,

THE BLACK WATCH returns! The men you found so intriguing are now joined by women who are also part of this secret organization created by BJ James. Look for them in *Whispers in the Dark*, this month's MAN OF THE MONTH.

Leanne Banks's delightful miniseries HOW TO CATCH A PRINCESS—all about three childhood friends who kiss a lot of frogs before they each meet their handsome prince—continues with *The You-Can't-Make-Me Bride*. And Elizabeth Bevarly's series THE FAMILY McCORMICK concludes with *Georgia Meets Her Groom*. Romance blooms as the McCormick family is finally reunited.

Peggy Moreland's tantalizing miniseries TROUBLE IN TEXAS begins this month with *Marry Me, Cowboy*. When the men of Temptation, Texas, decide they want wives, they find them the newfangled way—they *advertise!*

A Western from Jackie Merritt is always a treat, so I'm excited about this month's *Wind River Ranch*—it's ultrasensuous and totally compelling. And the month is completed with *Wedding Planner Tames Rancher!*, an engaging romp by Pamela Ingrahm. There's nothing better than curling up with a Silhouette Desire book, so enjoy!

Regards,

Lucia Macro

Senior Editor

Please address questions and book requests to:
Silhouette Reader Service
U.S.: 3010 Walden Ave., P.O. Box 1325, Buffalo, NY 14269
Canadian: P.O. Box 609, Fort Erie, Ont. L2A 5X3

BJ JAMES
WHISPERS IN THE DARK

SILHOUETTE *Desire*®
Published by Silhouette Books
America's Publisher of Contemporary Romance

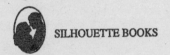

SILHOUETTE BOOKS

ISBN 0-373-76081-7

WHISPERS IN THE DARK

BJ JAMES

married her high school sweetheart straight out of college and soon found that books were delightful companions during her lonely nights as a doctor's wife. But she never dreamed she'd be more than a reader, never expected to be one of the blessed, letting her imagination soar, weaving magic of her own.

BJ has twice been honored by the Georgia Romance Writers with their prestigious Maggie Award for Best Short Contemporary Romance. She has also received the following awards from *Romantic Times:* Critic's Choice Award of 1994-1995, Career Achievement Award for Series Storyteller of the Year, and Best Desire of 1994-1995 for *The Saint of Bourbon Street.*

Two

A panther stalked the shadowy corridor. Dark, lean, silent. A sartorial contradiction in a black blazer neatly buttoned, trousers perfectly creased, and pearl gray shirt of immaculate detail. A tie of rough silk, loosened, drawn down a fraction from the open collar, completed an air of barbaric elegance.

The clinic had closed hours ago, the tranquility of deserted thoroughfares broken only by light steps and muted voices of the midnight shift. This handsome intruder could have been a concerned physician returning for late rounds at the end of a protracted evening out. One look into the wintry blaze of his startling green eyes was enough to warn that he was not.

The nurse in charge would have stopped him as he passed her by. Should have, but the pain in the brief glance he spared her nailed her immutably in her seat. The savagery of rage lying like a mask over his stark face made her more than grateful for the protective enclosure of her station.

As he moved beyond her bright island into the second shadowy extension of her floor, she stared after him, her mind a jumble of stunning, vivid impressions. Surely she was only imagining. But was she? Had she? Had she only imagined

him? The look? The manner? The man? Could anyone truly
be so uncivilized beneath an urbane veneer? His face? Did its
harsh lines rival chiseled stone? Could hair be that thick, that
dark? And which of a thousand clichés would describe it?
Blue-black? Iridescent? Soot? Did it blaze beneath the pale
light with silver fire?

Were any eyes so green? So desperate? So kind?

Kind?

"No!" Biting her lip, she struggled in a mental fugue, determined to convince herself of her mistake.

It was past midnight, she was tired. She was wrong. But
even that resolve faltered as her competent fingers, hovering
unsteadily over a hidden switch, curled, one by one, into her
palm. Security could continue in a ceaseless and rarely changing routine, she wouldn't be summoning them. If the breach
in protocol meant her job? What was a paycheck when one
faced a stalking brute looking for someone to eat?

"After all," she muttered as she picked up her pen, pretending to go about the business of charting the nightly needs
of her patients, "why put a paltry stumbling block in the path
of the inevitable?"

Why, indeed, she wondered as she waited and listened.

There was but one door past her station, one suite. But
Nurse Carstairs wouldn't have needed that obvious fact to
spell out the destination of this grave and formidable trans-
gressor. From the moment he'd stepped onto her hall, she'd
needed no bolt of mental lightning to divine that he'd come
in answer to a summons from the laird who waited and grieved
behind its closed door.

"They are as different as the sun from the moon," she
mused, putting her pen and pretense aside. Adding, without
really understanding, "Yet so much the same."

He was beyond her sight, this virile intruder into the world
of exquisitely specialized medicine. But, in the quiet, she
heard the ceasing of his nearly soundless step. A quick rap.
The scrape of a door. Then—shattering her new-found resolve
that she'd seen the prowling beast—the gentle ripple of his
deep voice.

"Patrick."

Forward

In desperate answer to a need prompted by changing times and mores, Simon McKinzie, dedicated and uncompromising leader of the Black Watch, has been called upon by the president of the United States to form a more covert and more dangerous division of his most clandestine clan. Ranging the world in ongoing assembly of this unique unit, he has gathered and will gather in the elite among the elite—those born with the gift or the curse of skills transcending the norm. Men and women who bring extraordinary and uncommon talents in answer to extraordinary and uncommon demands. They are, in most cases, men and women who have plummeted to the brink of hell because of their talents. Tortured souls who have stared down into the maw of destruction, been burned by its fires, yet have come back, better, surer, stronger. Driven and colder.

As officially nameless as The Black Watch, to those few who have had the misfortune and need of calling on their dark service, they are known as Simon's chosen...Simon's Marauders.

One

A telephone rang in the spartan mountain retreat. A telephone seldom used. Turning from a fire that did nothing to warm him in the unseasonable chill of late August, Simon McKinzie crossed with a heavy step to the jangling instrument. On the third ring, his square, strong hand raised the receiver slowly.

His massive shoulders were bowed, his face bleak. This was the call for which he'd been waiting. The call he'd feared.

"Yes?" No other greeting or identification was necessary, any informed of this line would not need it. Especially the man who called now.

"I heard. I've been waiting." With his back to spacious windows and Blue Ridge vistas heralding an early autumn, he listened.

"Is there no other way?" His bleak expression grew bleaker. "I see." The words were raw, bitter. Blunt fingers raked through silver hair, and, after a silent minute, he nodded. "I understand, and I agree."

Again there was a hush in the softly lit study. A hush broken only by the crackle of the fire, the tick of a clock, and the voice that recounted horror in his ear. And into a hollow still-

ess he pledged, "The one you need will be on the way within
the hour."

There was more. More Simon didn't need to hear, but out
of concern and respect, he listened. "Within the hour," he
repeated when the somber soliloquy was done. "You have my
word.

"And Jordana?" Hesitating, girding himself, he asked,
"How is she?"

This time, as he listened, even the fire seemed mute, the
clock still. A weighted sigh shredded his throat, and his voice
roughened in shared pain. "I'm here, should you need me. If
you need me."

Returning the receiver to its cradle, he sat at the edge of his
desk. As his hands curled around its beveled edge, his mind
filled with memories of a young wife and mother, her fragile
daughter, and the compelling man who loved them. And with
it came the desolation that only the powerful can know in the
face of utter helplessness.

Jordana, of whom Simon asked so earnestly and spoke so
lovingly, was Jordana Daniel McCallum. A beautiful woman,
a gentle woman. An American born to the power of wealth
and influence, wed to more of the same in McCallum, her wild
and wily auburn-haired Scot.

McCallum, chieftain of his clan, laird of her heart. Her true
beloved, tamed by none but his own beloved, and only because
he wished it.

McCallum, who fought as he lived, and loved as she—with
all his might, with all his heart.

Now, in this worst hour, even as one who built corporate
empires as a way of life, moved mountains as easily as others
moved hills of sand, and commanded the respectful friendship
of those as powerful, this man, this mighty Scot could do
nothing. As the woman he loved above all else lay injured,
perhaps dying, and with his family under siege, he had turned
in his hopelessness to those he trusted.

But there was still hope. There was a way.

And in the hush of his study, oblivious to towering vistas
and autumn chill, as he lifted the receiver again, a silvering
tear of a man became much more than sorrowing friend. Much
more than an ally. Within the beat of an aching heart, in quiet

wrath, Simon McKinzie was the revered and sovereign com
mander of the most unique organization in the world. Th
most proficient. The most dangerous. The most covert—Th
Black Watch.

"Hope, Clan McCallum," he murmured gravely as the con
nection was complete. "In the one I send you."

Somewhere in Virginia, on the shore of the Chesapeak
another telephone rang. A voice answered softly, commentin
on the beautiful day, thanking the caller for patronizing a busi
ness that did not exist, and inviting the statement of his need

Interrupting the pleasantries, drawing a ragged breath, wit
steel in his words Simon McKinzie began.

* * *

The massive Scot stumbled to his feet, not out of clumsiness
or the burden of his size, but from fatigue and worry. And
from more than forty-eight hours without sleep as he kept a
bedside vigil. His arms were iron bands enveloping the newcomer, but it was the smaller man whose whipcord strength
offered support.

"Rafe."

"Yes."

Rafe Courtenay had come to Phoenix and the clinic from
another country, another continent, in answer to a summons
from the only man in the world who commanded such loyalty
from the solitary Creole. Backing out of the desperate embrace, but keeping his hand on a taut shoulder, he looked up
at Patrick McCallum, his friend and chosen family for most
of his life.

If she could have seen, Nurse Carstairs would have been
shocked to know how astute she'd been, that she'd imagined
nothing. Rafe Courtenay and Patrick McCallum were, indeed,
as different as the sun from the moon. And, indeed, the same.
They were men of the same ilk, cast in the same mold. Dynamic, intense, complex and passionate. But individual. Distinctive. Different.

Out of the meshing of similarity, in the complement of difference, bonds stronger than mere friendship had grown. Trust,
complete, deep and abiding; honor, unflinching, unfaltering;
and in all of it, love. The love of brothers, among men who
had none, born in adolescence and their tenure in a most ex-
clusive, most private academy. Enduring into manhood and
the building of McCallum holdings into a corporate empire.
Meshing them into the most powerful and successful consor-
tium in the business world.

If Patrick—with fiery temperament, shrewd but impetuous
judgment and monumental strength—was head and heart of
McCallum International; Rafe—CEO of phenomenal intellect,
razor-edged insight and whipcord resilience—was its soul. Its
cool, quiet strength. Its solidarity.

Each was fire. Each was ice. In his own way.

And through the years, more times than either remembered
or bothered to count, the difference in one had served the
other. It would now. Looking long into the eyes of his friend,

Rafe saw him as few ever saw him. The keen, searching ap
praisal proved the Scot was on the edge, taxing even his Go
liath-like strength, but contending, as only he could, with the
threat to his family.

A moment of silent communication and a bare nod reaf
firmed a commitment, the joining of forces. From this mo
ment, in his fight for the life of his wife and his child, Patric
was not alone.

Together they moved to the bed, to the still, white figure o
the woman who lay like a sleeping princess waiting for he
prince. "How is she?" Rafe asked, his heart heavy with worr
for the only woman he'd ever trusted. The woman he coul
have loved, had Patrick not loved her first. "Has there bee
any change?"

Taking a bruised and scratched hand in his, Patrick laced
his fingers through Jordana's. "Beyond the trauma to her head
tests have shown she's in no immediate danger from interna
or external injuries, and no bones are broken. More than tha
assurance, nothing's changed."

"Any sign that she's coming out of the coma?"

"None." Even as he delivered the grim reply, Patrick
squeezed his wife's hand hoping for a response that neve
came. "Shortly after she was airlifted to the hospital in a semi
conscious state, she became agitated. When I arrived sh
calmed and lapsed into this deep sleep. Her doctors interpre
the shift in her behavior as an indication that, even with th
bruising and swelling in her brain, she knew I was with her
We don't know how much more she hears and understands
or what she remembers of the accident."

The oblique and unneeded warning did not go unperceived
Rafe wouldn't openly discuss or question the events surround
ing the present situation in any case. Nor did he need to b
told that the longer the coma continued, the deeper she sank
into it, the poorer Jordana's chances of recovery.

Touching Patrick's shoulder again, in an undertone, he said
"We need to talk."

"Yes." Releasing Jordana, Patrick bent to kiss her fore
head. "I need to speak with Rafe for a bit in private, sweet
heart," he murmured. "I won't be long, I promise."

As the two men stepped into the corridor, a nurse, wh

seemed to appear out of nowhere, slipped quietly into the room to take up the vigil. When Patrick was satisfied that all was well, he led Rafe to a small lounge hidden away in an alcove across from the door that led to Jordana's suite.

"All right," Rafe said as he set a cup of steaming coffee before Patrick and took a seat by him at the small table. "Tell me what happened."

Patrick's head reared back, his hollow eyes were wild and fierce, and more frightened than they'd ever been. "Jordana's been hurt, so terribly hurt, Rafe. And our daughter's been taken. I promised to take care of them and I didn't!"

"You have. You did."

"No! Somewhere, somehow, I did something wrong."

"You did nothing wrong, Patrick. Loving them more and protecting them better than anyone in the world could have isn't wrong."

"Except, this time, I failed them." Patrick's heavy shoulders slumped. "What if…" His eyes closed against the unthinkable. "Dear God! What would I do without them?"

"*Nothing!* You would do nothing without them. What you're thinking isn't going to occur."

"Rafe…"

"Tell me what happened, Patrick," Rafe insisted with a calming air of command. "Start from the beginning, don't leave out a single detail."

Patrick gripped the cup as if it were a lifeline, but didn't raise it to his lips. "There's not a lot to tell, that's the damnable part in this."

"Then tell what there is to tell. Begin with where and how."

Rafe would not give up, and, Patrick realized, would not let him give up. Drawing a long shuddering breath, he nodded. And, beneath the burden of his grief, shone the first glimmer of the return of the invincible Scot. "Jordana was taking Courtney to her morning dance class. A sort of mother-daughter day for them."

"Who was driving?"

"Ian, of course."

"Of course," Rafe expected that it would be Ian. It would have been unlikely anyone but the wizened Highlander, who had driven for the McCallums for years, would be entrusted to chauffeur Patrick's blind wife and his only daughter. His precious treasures.

"Was he injured?"

"He was dazed by the impact, and he'll be a little sore for a while, but nothing more."

"What did he see?" Intent, intense, Rafe leaned forward. "What can he tell us?"

"There was very little time to see anything. He was just turning onto the highway from the ranch when they were broadsided by a car hidden and waiting in a service road."

"Jordana's side taking the brunt of the impact," Rafe ventured the obvious.

As if he didn't hear, Patrick's voice droned on, relating the little he knew. "Three things happened almost consecutively. Ian unlocked the doors of the car and dashed to the back passenger's side, to Jordana. A passenger in the other vehicle bailed out and ran, leaving the driver who had not survived. While Ian was at the opposite side, a third accomplice ran from the underbrush. He grabbed Courtney from the back seat, shoved her into yet another hidden vehicle, and sped away. Presumably, with the one who escaped the crash and any one else who was involved."

"Son of a bitch!" Grave and troubled, Rafe's voice was strained. As he thought of his namesake, how tiny she was at four years, how frightened she would be, his look was laced with venom. "When did the ransom note arrive? How?"

"It didn't arrive, Rafe. It was left on the seat where Courtney sat."

"Planned down to the last hellish detail, with nothing left to chance." There was fire blazing in the normally cool Creole as he asked, bitterly, "How much?"

Patrick lifted a stricken gaze. "Not a penny."

Cold dread, gathering like a sickness in him, marked the harsh quirk of Rafe's lips. "Then what? And, damn their souls, why? Who are they? What do they want?"

"Why and what they want was outlined in excruciating detail in the note. Courtney was taken by members of a radical group that calls itself Apostles for a Better Day. She was chosen because of my friendship with Jim Brigman, and what they perceive as my prominence and political influence because he's governor." The Scot's face grew grimmer, paler, in startling contrast to the dark auburn of the curling, shaggy mane that framed it. "In exchange for my daughter they've demanded that, by that influence, I arrange and expedite the release of their leader from death row."

"Death row!" Shock upon shock levied its toll on an unprepared Rafe. "They must be out of their collective minds. Who is this man? What the hell is he?"

"A mad dog," Patrick said levelly. "A mad dog who calls himself Father Tomorrow and who kills in the name of his cause without a qualm."

"Zealots!" Rafe's decree was accompanied by a string of heated epithets. "Fanatics who twist whatever religion and whatever doctrine they espouse to accommodate themselves. The most deadly and unpredictable element in society."

Pushing away his cup and kicking back the chair too small for his bulk, Patrick lurched to his feet. Despite the vicious motion, helplessness and defeat were apparent in every line of his body. "I've spoken with Jim."

Something in his look and tone chilled Rafe even more. "And?"

"No go." Arms crossed over his chest, his back to the lounge, Patrick glared out a window at a night as black as his thoughts. "A proven killer can't be released. Even if there was a question of guilt, the man is unstable and too dangerous. Granting his freedom would be tantamount to unleashing a monster. Jim has pledged his help in any way possible, but he dares not turn such an unconscionable creature loose on the public." His arms crossed tighter, his fingers crumpled the fabric of his shirt. "Not for Courtney. Not for anyone.

"I could give them millions, castles, islands." There were tears on Patrick's face, but he made no effort to wipe them away. "An empire is theirs for the asking, with not one regret for its loss. Yet, with all I have, I can't give what they've demanded. The one thing that would free my little girl."

"All right. If we can't give them what they want for Courtney, we do it the hard way. We take her back without it." Rafe would not waste another thought on bitter recriminations, or sympathy that Patrick neither wanted nor needed. He addressed the crux of the situation instead. "How much time do we have?"

"We had five days."

"Had?"

"Tomorrow marks the beginning of the last three."

Glancing at his watch, discovering, for the first time in his concern, that tomorrow had become today, Rafe said nothing.

"We know where Courtney's being held."

Patrick's wooden statement shattered Rafe's calm demeanor as nothing else. "What the hell? You know where she is? How?"

"The Apostles made no effort to cover their tracks. Their trail was so obvious, it was thought to be a ruse in the beginning. Then it became apparent they wanted us to know, and to understand how impossible rescue would be."

"Where is she, Patrick?" Rafe asked directly, his tone calm but savage.

"The men who took Courtney were tracked into the high desert north of Sedona by a specially trained unit of rangers called in by the governor. At some point she was handed over to one man, who took her the rest of the way to a mountain. Hell!" Patrick slammed a fist on the table. "It's worse than a mountain. It's a monstrous aberration among aberrations. A spike of land as barren as the devil's own, and no one can climb it without being seen."

The trilling burr of Scotland was thick in Patrick's diatribe, recalling the lush and craggy highlands of his homeland. A land he loved only a bit more than the land he decried in the extremity of distress. "The surrounding terrain and the old miner's shack at its peak constitute a veritable fortress." The growling trill grew more pronounced. "A natural, impregnable stronghold."

"You were intended to believe rescue is impossible, but is it? Is anything truly impregnable? There's always a way, and we'll find it, Patrick. There lies our hope."

"Maybe."

The Scot turned stiffly toward the door of the softly lit suite, and something in his manner told the man who knew him so well that way had already been found. Rafe waited, biding his time.

"Maybe there is a way." Patrick's head moved from side to side, bemused, dejected. "But I can't leave Jordana. If she's aware at all and I'm not here, she'll know something terrible is wrong. The stress might be all that's needed to…"

With a hand at Patrick's wrist, Rafe stopped the anguish of a man torn between two loves. "You see to Jordana, I'll do what's needed to bring Courtney home."

"You can't." The answer came quickly, flatly. "There are circumstances and conditions you don't understand. For once, Rafe, even you can't do the impossible. But Simon has someone who can, someone he's sending. Our last resort." Patrick turned again to the window, stared again, blindly, into the darkness. But in his mind there were barren, ragged peaks shrouded by the night. "Our one chance. Our only hope."

"Then I'll help Simon's man bring her home," Rafe promised.

Though Patrick spoke of hope, there had never been such melancholy in his voice. Not when he was thirteen, deserted by his faithless mother, failed by his grieving father and consigned to exile in a strange school, in a strange country. Lost and alone among a strange people, he had not been like this. Not even the ultimate death of his father wreaked such suffering upon him. Silently Rafe vowed he would take away the pain, and give back the hope—along with the littlest Mc-Callum.

"Three days, Patrick," he murmured hoarsely. "I promise."

"You won't do anything irrational?" What Patrick left unspoken was his wish that if the impossible were truly that, if one tragedy, or two, were inevitable, there needn't be a third.

"No more than you would." A crooked grin lifted the corner of Rafe's mouth, but left his eyes unchanged. As Patrick had been before his marriage, the Creole was an accomplished sportsman and adventurer. There was little he hadn't tried, little he hadn't dared. When time and McCallum International permitted, his idea of relaxing was to battle the elements in one form or another. This time, in a life or death struggle, the stakes would be higher—a life other than his own.

"I promise to do no more and no less than you would, my friend," Rafe mused softly. "In the same circumstance."

For a moment their eyes met and held. Patrick nodded, slowly, grimly, and on that understanding returned to his seat.

Less than a quarter hour later, strategy outlined, each lurid detail and fact branded on his mind, Rafe left Patrick. In the next three days, while the Scot fought for the life of his wife, the Creole would go to the mountains, to fight in his stead.

Rafe Courtenay would go to do battle for the life of the beloved daughter of his chosen brother. For his own namesake. For his godchild.

For Courtney...the love of his warrior's heart.

Three

The scene that greeted Rafe was alien, a surreal backdrop from a science fiction movie. Glaring yellow lights, falling on red rock and flying dust, lent an eerie sense of otherworldliness to the camp and its cluster of trucks and tents hunkered in the stark, rocky basin. He could, he thought, just as easily be looking down on the landscape of Mars as the high desert of Arizona.

When he dropped to the ground, waving the hovering helicopter bearing the logo of McCallum International back into the night sky, he knew no place had ever been more real. Nothing he'd ever done as important.

"Mr. Courtenay, sir." The shout of the young man, who addressed him from the edge of a boil of orange fog, could barely be heard above the whine of the chopper's engine.

Ducking, small backpack in hand, Rafe dashed from the whipping lash of the revving rotors. As he approached, the young ranger smiled briefly and took the bag from him. "Glad you could make it, sir."

His handshake was firm, his uniform amazingly neatly pressed into smooth surfaces and sharp creases. Only his face was rumpled from lack of sleep. The tag clipped to the breast pocket of his shirt confirmed he was Joe Collins, a second before he introduced himself.

"I've been assigned to serve as your liaison, to familiarize you with the camp and procure whatever else you feel you need," he continued as he escorted Rafe to his tent. As they passed by, busy people, dressed as Joe was dressed, with faces as strained and harried, acknowledged the newcomer. With only a nod or wave of greeting they returned to the work that engrossed them.

"As you will see, sir," Joe said as he stopped by one in a line of smaller tents, "we have an excellent Search and Rescue team. But this is a little beyond our field of expertise."

The last was said apologetically. Rafe responded succinctly, "This is a little beyond anyone's field of expertise, Ranger Collins."

"Yes, sir. Thank God."

"Indeed," Rafe agreed as he scanned the camp again, noting the propitious arrangement, the equipment, including detailed maps spread over a bevy of tables near a powerful radio. Parked at one side were a half dozen all-terrain vehicles that had seen hard and recent use. Opposite, and set a little apart, was a small remuda. He slanted a questioning look at his guide. "Horses?"

"Yes, sir. A good portion of the terrain we've covered is accessible only by horseback. Some of it too bad even for them. Even in relays." Setting down the bag, he shrugged, a move at odds with his perfect posture. "The gun who was brought in thinks at least part of what we walked and climbed can be crossed by a horse. A particular horse. A stallion trucked in just before you arrived."

"What horse would that be?" Interest stirred, Rafe waited for his answer.

"Black Jack, from The Broken Spur."

Feeling the first real frisson of encouragement since he'd seen the desolation around him, Rafe nodded his approval. Black Jack was a magnificent creature of no little reputation among horsemen and breeders such as Patrick. The stallion had made news by accomplishing the unthinkable more than once, and only a rider of incomparable skill could handle him.

"If this gun, as you call him, knows his stuff as well as he knows his horses, maybe we have a chance to make this work."

"Maybe." The answer was noncommittal, but the look Joe Collins shot at Rafe was edged with surprise.

"You were right about your Search and Rescue team. From what Patrick told me nothing has been left undone. But now there is one more thing I'll require." Taking a pen and small notebook from the inside pocket of his jacket, Rafe scribbled a name and telephone number. "Call this number, ask for Tyree." Tearing the page from the notebook he handed it to Collins. "Tell him I need El Mirlo immediately, then give him specific directions to the camp."

"Yes, sir." Collins jumped to attention, Rafe half expected he would salute. "El Mirlo. The Blackbird." There was awe in the younger man's tone as he translated the Spanish name of the horse nearly as distinguished as Blackjack. "I'll see to it right away."

"One more thing before you go." Scanning the task force, Rafe detained the ranger with those few short words before he could race away. "The gun, where is he?"

Joe Collins gave him the same odd look he had before, a light flush staining his cheeks. "She, sir," he managed at last, as if he weren't sure how his answer would be received. Taking a fold of papers from a hip pocket he offered them to Rafe. "I was instructed to give you this, a dossier explaining who she is."

Halting in the act of slipping the notebook back in his jacket, Rafe took the papers from him, tucking them away, as well, without a glance. His narrow look swept over the ranger, pinning him in place. "She?"

"Yes, sir." Another uneasy shrug. "We thought you knew."

"Do you have a problem with that, Mr. Courtenay?"

Rafe's turn was slow, measured, the gaze that only seconds ago had held the ranger in place, swept over the woman who stood a half dozen paces away. And though there was no reason to think he'd ever seen her before, nor any woman resembling her, he was struck by a strong sense of déjà vu. A sensation to be explored later, rather than now, as he turned his undeterred regard on her.

Instead of the common uniform, she was in civilian dress. Boots, jeans, Western shirt, the customary Stetson. He noted she wore a holstered Colt belted at her hip, and no spurs on her boots.

"You move very quietly," he observed softly as he finished his perusal.

"What you mean is I move very quietly, for a woman." There was no rancor in her voice. One look warned she had little time or patience with petty angers.

"What I meant," Rafe replied patiently, "is what I said. You move very quietly, for anyone."

A slight bow afforded him the point. "Should I say thank you?"

"You don't strike me as a woman who would waste her breath on false platitudes."

She chuckled quietly, the humor genuine, giving him another point. "Just how do I strike you, Mr. Courtenay?"

Rafe was not surprised that she knew him. The camp as a whole had been informed by Patrick that he was coming, and what he would expect. "That would require some thought and consideration."

The laugh again, low, smoky. In the right place, the right circumstance, a little sexy. "Of course," she agreed. "But you're a quick study, aren't you, Mr.—"

"Rafe. From you, I prefer Rafe."

"If you like." By her manner she told him his name was of so little consequence at the moment, she would call him George, if he liked. "Now, Rafe." She moved a step closer. "About that quick study."

Letting her feel the weight of his scrutiny, he took her measure slowly, with a piercing thoroughness. Another woman might have flinched or blushed, facing such total invasion of her person. But not this one. He liked that, found it challenging, as he drew his study out more than was needed. After a long, long moment, in which Joe Collins's gaping attention bounced like a racket ball between them, Rafe's gaze returned to settle on her face.

"All done?" She stood with her hands at her hips, her feet apart, her chin jutted an unmistakable fraction.

"For now." A cryptic answer, drawing little reaction. She was a cool one.

Her head tilted a bit, a brow lifted. "Well?"

"Do you want the particulars?"

"However you like it, Mr. Courtenay."

"Rafe," he reminded.

"Rafe," she parroted in droll concession.

Silence fell like a gauntlet. Joe Collins stared and waited. Rafe was first to react. "All right," he mused, tugging the tie he hadn't taken time to remove down another notch. "The particulars, as I see them. You're five-five, without the boots, and weigh, maybe, one fifteen with them. Shoulder-length hair. Dark brown, if not black, maybe with a hint of red in sunlight. On a bet, a little unruly at times. Tied, at the moment, with whatever was handy. On the trail, I suspect it will be tucked under the Stetson."

He waited for the slight acknowledging bow of her head then resumed a concise cataloging of her features. "Oval face, high cheekbones. Fine-textured skin, a tint that suggests it tans easily and rarely burns. A nose with a slight deviation. From a break, I would surmise. Brows, arched and fine, dark as night.

"Your eyes..." He paused only to draw a breath. "In this garish light I can't say, but too dark for blue or gray, too pale for true brown. Possibly the color of old sherry?" It was a question that begged no answer as he moved on to finer, surer points. "A belligerent chin that telegraphs your moods, and a mouth made for smiling."

In a short pause in the tabulation, there was a clash of gazes. One chin angled another inch. Neither man nor woman smiled.

With a restrained quirk of his lips Rafe returned to his commentary. "As Simon would expect and demand, you're obviously in good physical condition. A little slender. Yet, I would wager, strong for your size. You've a trim figure, a little boyish for my taste, but appealing."

Dragging in another, slower breath, his unwavering gaze probing the shadows cast by the Stetson, he murmured, "And no matter how you dress down, no man in his right mind would ever forget you're a woman." The quirk became a small smile playing over his face. "Shall I go on, Miss…?"

"O'Hara," Joe Collins interjected, flustered that in his pre-occupation he'd been remiss in common courtesy. "Valentina," he finished lamely. Both their names has been buzzed through the camp. She'd had the advantage of learning of Rafe Courtenay from camp gossip and speculation.

"O'Hara," Rafe mused aloud over the name. It suited her to be Irish. It suited very well. "Shall I go on, then, Miss O'Hara?"

"By all means," she responded with the first hint of strained grace. "Perhaps you'd like to look at my teeth, to judge my age."

Rafe allowed himself a chuckle. "No need. Your face and body say you're twenty-two. You're eyes say thirty-two, thirty-three. I put my trust in the eyes."

"Touché." Another point for this man who had become her quiet adversary. "An excellent guess. I'm thirty-three."

Turning, moving toward the tent she'd just left, she stopped at a table set before it. Carefully, she lifted a cloth covering a dismantled rifle. The oiled barrel was gleaming ebony under the yellow lights; the polished stock, warm mahogany. The tool of a perilous trade, and well cared for.

Her fingers trailed familiarly over burnished wood, curled briefly around the trigger, then lifted from it. Dropping the cloth over the weapon again, she faced him once more as abruptly as she'd turned away. "You disappoint me, Mr. Courtenay."

"How so, Miss O'Hara?" They were back to formalities, the fencing was over, the gloves were off. "Disappointing you is the last thing I'd want to do."

Valentina laughed. There was wry amusement in its inflection, and in her demeanor. "What you've described any eye or any mirror could tell. I expected better from you. More insight. More depth."

"Perhaps I choose to keep my deeper perceptions to myself."

"What? No detailed questioning of the logistics? No reservations about my skill? No sly wondering if I can really make the shot to free Patrick McCallum's daughter?"

"I don't need to question, or wonder. I have no reservations. Not about the logistics or your skill, O'Hara. Because I know Patrick McCallum, I know every alternate avenue has been closed, leaving only the one recourse. I repeat, because I know Patrick, I understand and trust there's no other way to save his daughter but to put her life in the hands of one person. Because I know Simon McKinzie, because you are his choice, I know you're the best, the only one, for the job.

"I don't need your credentials." Quietly, he reiterated his point, closing the subject. "That this is Patrick's decision, and you are Simon's choice, is enough."

"Except that you plan one small change."

"Yes. I'm going with you." She did not react, and he felt no surprise that she would have drawn this conclusion from the bit of conversation she'd overheard. In his mind the reasoning was only logical. "I go in Patrick's stead, for Courtney and Jordana. And for myself."

"You're mistaken," Valentina contradicted flatly. "No one goes. I ride alone. I work alone."

"Not this time."

"This time above all." Dismissing Rafe, forestalling any protest he might lodge, without a glance, she walked past him. Pausing briefly by the ranger, she murmured, "Joey, the call to Tyree won't be necessary. Mr. Courtenay won't be needing El Mirlo."

"Yes, ma'am." Joe Collins didn't speak again, nor did Rafe, while each watched her take the path to the separate corral that cordoned the stallion.

As she approached the temporary fence, the skittish Black Jack, renowned for both his sure feet and savage temperament, snorted and danced away. From his place Rafe could hear, but not distinguish, the words of her singsong croon as she sought to calm and entice the stallion to her.

Rearing, hooves flashing at the air, the horse squealed his displeasure at unfamiliar surroundings and strange people. Valentina did not flinch, her quiet tone did not change. Black Jack raced the length of the back fence. He pawed the dust and tossed his rippling mane. Ears flattened, nostrils flaring, he paced, he pranced, he ignored the woman.

In response, her tone rose a degree. Assuring, calming, it

floated across the clearing. "Having a little temper tantrum, are you? I'm not sure I blame you. I wouldn't like to be cooped up in a strange place, with strange people, any more than you do. But it doesn't have to be that way. It isn't that way. I'm here...and we've met before."

The stallion quieted, stared away from the hand she extended. Her song dropped again to a low murmur, her hand was steady. Black Jack snorted, his ears flicked, his head turned to her. He took a tentative step, paused, snorted again, and took another. Stretching out his neck, he nibbled curiously at her fingers. His velvet muzzle roamed over her gently curling hand and nudged at her arm. Quivering, he stood as she stroked him. Then, with a low wicker, he moved, crowding the fence to snuffle at her cheek.

"Well, I'll be damned," Rafe muttered in an undertone.

"Yes, sir." Joe Collins exhaled a long held breath. "Me, too."

And, in that moment, it all clicked into place. Rafe understood the sense of familiarity. He'd never met Valentina O'Hara, but he'd seen her face many times. It had been years since she'd been an Olympian, sweeping the gold in her fields of choice. First with her skill with a rifle, then with her riding. The name he'd forgotten had been on every tongue, for no woman before her had accomplished as much. And none since.

For a time she was the darling of the media, a household word, the season's wonder. Then, electing not to cash in on her fame, shunning a fortune in endorsements and advertising, she had, quite simply, dropped out of sight.

She'd been nineteen then, Rafe remembered as he watched her. Intrigued, he wondered where she'd been for the past fourteen years? What had she done? How had her path crossed with Simon's? Why? When?

He had no answers. Perhaps he would find some of them in the dossier given to him by Joe Collins. Some, he suspected, not all. Not the answers that really mattered. But, he vowed, he would have them, before this was done.

"Make the call, Joe," he said abruptly. "Tell Tyree to meet me at sunup. Not here, but at the wash a half mile north of the basin. Tell him the old map in Patrick's study identifies it as the Hacker homestead."

He had given the order without looking away from the stallion and the woman. Now he turned his face to the sky. "It will be dawn soon. I need to be briefed, and there's a lot of planning left to do before first light."

"Yes, sir," Joe put in smartly. With a quick salute, eager to make amends for the blunder in introductions, he launched into the task.

Rafe watched the ranger till he was out of sight before he turned again to the corral. Concern etched his face, uneased by the sureness and rapport established between the stallion and the woman. She was a champion, an expert rider, a phenomenal shot, and one of Simon's chosen.

But would it be enough?

"Can anyone do this? God help you, lady, can you?" Wheeling about, he stalked to the tent that was his. Catching back the flap that covered the entrance, he paused, his gaze drawn again to her.

"Sunup, O'Hara," he pledged grimly. "And, like it or not, you and your new pet stallion will have company on the trail and the mountain. Then we'll see."

His grip on the flap was hard and desperate. "God help us both, we'll see."

"The shack is here." In the weak, first light of dawn, augmented by the yellow glow of lanterns, Richard Trent, Commander of Search and Rescue Operations, tapped his pointer against a map mounted on a stand. "The only possible trail is here, and it's virtually as inaccessible as the rest of the ground. We could make short work of this by helicopter. That is, if we dared. Which we don't. These people, who call themselves Apostles for a New Day, are certifiable nuts. The unstable fringe of an unstable fringe, each a little crazier than the last. The one thing we can count on is that they do what they promise."

Taking the pointer from the map, he held it before him, his grip threatening to snap it. "If they say the little girl will be killed at the first hint of intrusion, she will be."

"You're certain there's only one person guarding her?" Until now Valentina had been content to stand a little apart, listening, asking no questions. "I'll be lucky to get one shot. Two would be asking for a miracle."

"Dead certain. One man. That much we've proven from surveillance. His name is Edmund Brown." Laying aside the pointer, the commander tipped back the brim of his hat. "But don't derive too much relief from the fact that he's alone. Next to Father Tomorrow, *Brother* Brown is the most sadistic in their cult. Before he found religion he collected a string of convictions and arrests on a number of charges, ranging from attempted murder to petty theft.

"He was always skating on the edge of insanity. We have reason to believe the association with the Apostles finally tipped the scales."

Valentina left her place. Threading through the gathered group, she made her way to the front. Arms folded, eyes narrowed, she studied the exquisitely detailed and graphic map. She was knowledgeable about the land in general, but not specifically. "This peak," with a short cut nail she tapped the spot as she addressed the commander, "it has the best vantage point?"

"For the distance you would require, yes."

"What sort of cover does it offer?"

"Some scrub, but mostly rock."

"If he should see me?" She turned an unwavering gaze on the commander.

Richard Trent did not hesitate. "He'll kill the girl and then himself."

Valentina's sigh signaled her understanding of the gravity of the challenge she faced. "Then I'll just have to make sure he doesn't see me."

Rafe, who had been as content to listen, listened acutely to Valentina's responses. A map and a woman had done what a thousand words couldn't do. For until now, despite his quick study of the circumstance and Patrick's own maps, he hadn't fully comprehended the monstrous complications that lent the word impossible to the desperate gamble.

If they were to succeed, the key was this woman. Courtney's life was literally in Valentina O'Hara's hands.

The hands of an unlikely assassin.

And Rafe Courtenay would be by her side every step of the way.

Under the watchful eyes of the camp, Valentina led Black Jack from the corral. With her gear stored in bulging saddle-bags, a bedroll snapped at the back of the saddle, a Winchester and its case strapped to the front, her preparations were complete.

She was ready to ride.

"Val." Richard Trent approached her cautiously. He, as much as the rest of the camp, was astonished at her control over the stallion. But he didn't trust it would last through any startling moves. When she halted and stood looking up at him, her impatience evident, he embarked on his last-minute warning. "Remember, this man is worse than dangerous."

"I think you've suitably impressed that on me, Richard."

"Don't try to outthink him. And don't even begin to think you can outguess him. In a pressure situation, he won't know from one minute to the next what he'll do himself."

Valentina stirred restively, anxious to have done with this. Now that there was enough light to see the trail, it was time for talk to end and action to begin. "You sound like Simon."

"There are worse people to emulate."

"Certainly," she agreed. "There are." Swinging into the saddle, she looked down at Trent. "Don't worry, he taught me well. I wouldn't be here if there was anyone better."

In the watching crowd, someone coughed. Black Jack jumped and backed away, fighting the reins and Valentina. Leaning over his neck, riding light in the saddle, she stroked him, soothing him with whispered words only he could hear. In a matter of seconds the stallion was quiet again.

"Damn horse," Richard Trent groused. "He'll kill you before you ever get to the shack."

"No, he won't," Valentina replied as she overheard the comment she was not meant to hear. "We'll be fine when it's just the two of us."

"About that," Richard braved a step closer. "A couple of us could ride along for the first two days. Make it easier going on you for that time, then back off at the last."

"We've been through that time and again." She kept her voice low, but the impatient emphasis was there. "I ride alone, I work alone. Even if I didn't normally, this time I would. I must. You just see to it the men who are there now, surrounding the base of the peak, are ready to move in on a minute's notice. That's all they may have, a minute."

"Val..."

"No, Richard," she said firmly. "We can't risk any chance that there might be spotters in the vicinity who would connect me with Search and Rescue. If I'm seen, they have to think I'm just a rancher, or a dude, out for a ride. Someone they needn't be concerned about."

"When you're on foot? What then?"

"When I go to ground, no one will see me. I guarantee it." Curbing her irritation, she tried to speak moderately, when she wanted to shout and be done with this. "Richard, no one else can go."

"I know that's the way we said we'd do it."

"And that's the way we'll keep it." Black Jack danced away again. This time not in fright, but in eagerness to run. Drawing him to a stand, Valentina leaned down, offering her hand to the commander. "Wish me luck."

Richard Trent took her hand in his. His face was grim with worry as he looked up at her. He'd known her less than twenty-four hours. In those hours he'd learned to like her as a friend, as someone he'd like to know better. He respected her and trusted her judgment.

She was right. The reasonable part of him knew it. But this was his country, these were his people, his charges. Protecting them was his job. It did not set well with him to let her go into jeopardy while he stayed. "Val..."

Taking her hand from his, she cut him short. "Time's wasting. The temperature's rising."

"Dammit! I'd pull rank if I could."

"But you can't. You have no authority over special agents. Certainly none over me." Softly, she said again, "Wish me luck, Richard. I need it, you know."

Lips pursed, a hard held breath released, he nodded grimly. "Luck."

"Thanks." She laughed and tossed her braid from her

shoulders. "I'll see you in three days. No," she corrected. "We'll see you in three days. Courtney and I."

Touching spurs to Black Jack's glistening flank, she set him into an easy canter. At the entrance of the natural basin, she drew the stallion to a halt. Turning in the saddle she scanned the camp and the crew. But no eyes blazing green fire looked back at her.

"Strange," she murmured. "I thought…" Shrugging aside the thought she couldn't complete, she lifted a hand only an instant before she turned the stallion in a whirl. Then, giving him his head, she let him run.

"Three days," Richard Trent said as she disappeared from view. "Both of you. Child and woman, God willing."

As if sensing the need in her, the stallion ran as he hadn't in a long while. Black mane streaking behind him, tail high, his hooves pounded the hard-packed ground, taking the rough with the smooth as if there were no difference. Crouching low in the saddle, offering no resistance, Valentina urged him on.

There would be time for caution later. But, for now, it suited her purpose to be seen, as if she were someone just passing through in a hurry. Leaning even lower and dropping the reins, she caught Black Jack's mane, letting him run as he would. Her body rocked smoothly, gracefully, in concert with the horse, as if they were one. "That's us, boy, just passing through."

Needing no urging, Black Jack skidded down a wash and back up the other side with hardly a break in stride. Gaining level ground, racing his own shadow, he sped across the desert. Once more, with no change in his pace, he responded to the tug at his mane. Veering from the flat land, he made the turn that would begin the climb toward the cabin.

Dust stirred by the stallion had scarcely begun to settle as a second horse and rider burst through a clump of stunted trees at the wash. El Mirlo slid to a halt, dancing in his impatience as he obeyed the saw of the reins. Soothing him with a touch of his hand, Rafe stared after the figures fading rapidly into the distance.

"Irish," he muttered angrily as he held his mount in check,

"before you get where you're going, you'll break your reckless neck and the stallion's." As he glared after them they climbed higher. Small dots on the face of a hillside that would only grow steeper. "Your neck, for sure. And maybe mine."

El Mirlo snorted and reared, backing futilely away from the inescapable control of the reins. Rafe rode easy in the saddle, his anger giving way to intemperance.

"What the hell."

The low rumble accompanied a lash of the reins as he spurred his frenzied mount on. Scrambling up the side of the wash and over the top, grim rider in tow, the gelding that gleamed as darkly in the sun as Black Jack, galloped furiously into a dusty wake.

Four

"**F**ool woman."

As he began the climb himself, and even as the words erupted from his lips, Rafe knew he was wrong. What Valentina O'Hara was doing was simply natural, a part of her skill, a very significant part of her mission. If there were observers to report to the Apostles, even the most astute would see only a rider passing through. Never a dude, as she'd suggested, but an accomplished horsewoman riding for the sake of riding, feeling her oats.

No one would connect her with the camp, or Search and Rescue, for she'd left the basin by a difficult trail most would call impassable. Then, ranging widely on trailless terrain even more difficult, she'd come full circle miles from camp to begin the ride for Courtney McCallum's life.

Rafe's ride had been as circumventive. With Joe Collins's help he'd made his rendezvous with Tyree, and with El Mirlo had begun the race to intersect Valentina O'Hara's path. Tyree, who knew the country like an Indian scout, had reckoned correctly. The timing had been perfect. For now Rafe would hold back, keeping her barely in sight as she began the serious climb, weaving, dodging, picking a natural trail among red rocks.

If there were posted observers, they would see only a second rider, not as skilled, not as well mounted. A friend hoping to join her. Or better, lovers riding apart to a clandestine high desert tryst.

"Takes all kinds." His lip curled in distaste. In another environment he might have been tempted, but not in this. This was Courtney's life, and perhaps Jordana's. Both held in the balance by the expertise of a cold and calculating woman.

Rafe knew the type. There had been many such women in his life. Compassionless professionals to whom success was god. Who played hard and ruthlessly, as heartlessly as they worked. Users seeking success for the sake of power; and sex for the sake of gratification without the ritual of romance or entangling emotion. He'd finished with that breed, Valentina O'Hara's sisterhood, long ago.

"But I'll use you," he promised as he watched her take the horse through an impossible path and disappear behind an outcropping of stone. "Whatever it takes for Courtney, I'll do."

Urging El Mirlo from camouflaging scrub, he guided the gelding over the path Black Jack had taken. There was no time to think, or project, or even for distaste as a difficult ride deteriorated. Together, they slipped and slid, in constant danger of falling. Climbing ever upward.

The trail was a winding channel through and over stone. A converging animal crossing, from den or burrow to watering hole and stream. Gradually, as it became as much maze as animal track, he lost sight of her. But for one who had hunted bayous and swamps, tracking the only shod quadruped to pass through a dry and dusty land in ages was not difficult. The stallion's scramble was marked by trodden plants, dislodged pebbles and scarred stone. Rafe had only to find them.

Intent, concentration riveted, eyes and mind attuned to the discovery of the next mark of passage, Rafe drew to a startled halt as Black Jack and his rider stepped into his own path, blocking his way.

"That's far enough, Mr. Courtenay." Reins looped over the fingers of one hand, a forearm resting on her thigh, Valentina stared down the incline at him. "I'd be obliged if you'd be accommodating and go back now."

"Sorry." The empty apology tripped off his tongue out of habit. "I can't oblige or accommodate in this. I wouldn't if I could."

"You can," Valentina insisted. "We have a short window of time, every minute counts. You'll slow me down, waste precious seconds. You have already."

His mount stamped and snorted restlessly, eager to move again. Rafe calmed him with a touch. "It's you who wastes time. Give it up, O'Hara, nothing will persuade me to turn back."

Valentina's eyes were cold beneath the brim of her Stetson. "I can do this, Mr. Courtenay. I'm going to do it. And I'll do it better alone."

"I expect you can, lady. I expect you will," Rafe snapped, tiring of the debate. "But not alone. It's my goddaughter Brown is holding hostage, and I'll be there when you do what you must to free her."

Valentina cut her losses. She had no time and even less desire to debate than he. "You refuse to be rational, don't you?"

"Your idea of rationality, not mine."

"If you can't keep up, I won't wait for you." With a man the caliber of Rafe Courtenay, her threat would fall on deaf ears. But she had to try. "If you get into trouble, I'll leave you behind without a backward glance."

A muscle jerked in his cheek, his eyes narrowed. Deep in the brush a creature moved stealthily, eager that they move on. "I'll keep up, O'Hara." The guttural promise was short and grim. "And out of trouble."

"If you're counting on the horse to do the work for you, don't. The Blackbird is an extraordinary animal." She chose the English translation over Spanish. "So extraordinary Patrick McCallum should be held accountable for gelding him. Just remember, when the trail gets really rough, he'll only be as good as his rider."

Rafe nodded curtly. "Where you take Black Jack, I'll take El Mirlo. That's a promise."

"Fine!" Valentina's check on her temper slipped. "Do as

Wheeling Black Jack around in a tight turn, she leaned low as he responded to a touch of her heels, scrambling like a mountain goat up the ever steeper incline. She didn't look back, and wouldn't have in any case, but there was no need. The clash of El Mirlo's hooves over stone sounded with the knell of a bell at her back.

Rafe Courtenay could ride, and the Spanish gelding was truly as extraordinary as the reputation he'd established. But there was much worse to come. Eventually, if the interloper kept up, out of necessity and the need for secrecy they would go to ground, covering the remainder of the route on foot.

But, though a difficult trail grew more demanding, that time had not come, and she put the fortunes of Rafe Courtenay from her mind. The terrain and Black Jack required all her thoughts, her complete concentration. Hunching lower over his great bowed neck, she clung to his mane, urging him on. The same quiet chant that calmed him in the corral, the same gentle touch that enticed him, guided him now. With his great heart he responded.

Where Valentina led, Rafe followed, and the remainder of the day's ride was silent. Only the scrape and clatter of hooves and the creak of leather marked their passage.

Like a great ball of fire the sun burned in the sky, and the day grew hotter. Higher elevations brought no respite as dust churned and prickly brush clawed and clung. Sweat plastered her shirt to shoulders and breasts, and trickled into her eyes. Valentina tugged her hat lower, blinked away the sting of salt, and rode harder.

A little girl waited.

Sparing a glance from his own tribulations, Rafe saw her hardship and her dismissal. "One tough lady," he reminded himself when no reminder was needed. "With a heart as tough."

The comment was the last he would make in the hours to come. All his energies were expended in keeping his mount on the hillside and himself in the saddle. Engrossed in his battle, he was hardly aware when they topped a rise and the land flattened into a plateau. As suddenly, they were surrounded by a lush stand of pine. Tall sentinels in thick, scattered ranks, keeping an eternal watch.

Through a winding avenue encompassed by uncanny silence, weary riders and wearier mounts trod over shorn grass. A fragrant carpet, grazing for deer and range cattle. Beyond the stand, one beginning as abruptly as the other ended, lay a small tract of land within a walled enclosure. A sheltered, picturesque expanse, as welcoming as the land before was inhospitable. As cloistered as it had been naked. As temperate as the trail was brutal.

Clustered along a stream meandering lazily through this sky-high canyon were small groves of oak and maple, followed by mahogany and aspen. Each offering a welcome shield from the thrust of the sun. Where the stream was quietest and the shade deepest, Valentina dismounted. Kneeling on a stone, shoulder to shoulder with Black Jack, she drank the clear, sparkling water.

Dismounting with the stiffness of grueling hours in the saddle, Rafe followed suit, grateful for the respite.

As she led her reluctant mount from the stream, Valentina was pleased when he did the same. Taking care, as she had, that his horse not not drink too much, too quickly.

"We'll camp here for the night." With the speed of long habit, she unbuckled the cinch, lifting saddle and blanket from Black Jack.

"There's daylight left. Plenty of it," Rafe interjected. "We could make a number of miles before dark."

"There is, and we could." The saddle lay at the base of a stone. She flung the blanket over another to dry. "But this is it for the day."

Rafe's first inclination was to dispute the decision. But like her or not, he'd begun to respect Valentina O'Hara. The trail was a great leveler, a great teacher, and following in her path he'd learned every move had purpose. Every decision had been a judgment call. And each a sound one.

As she gathered grass to scrub the sweat from the stallion's back, he nodded abruptly. "All right."

Valentina stopped in mid-stroke, surprise showing through her guarded expression. "All right? You're agreeing, just like that?"

"Just like that." Rafe dispatched El Mirlo's saddle with an expertise rivaling her own. Lifting the horse's hooves he inspected for lodged pebbles or stone bruises. Then, running his hand from withers to hock, he checked for sprains or scrapes before gathering grass himself.

Val watched him in a mingling of approval and suspicion. "No argument?"

"No."

"No questions?"

"No questions." Rafe halted, regarding her thoughtfully before continuing his ministrations to El Mirlo. "I expect you'll tell me your reasons for stopping," he murmured almost silently. "In your own good time."

Valentina had the grace to feel ashamed. Certainly, she didn't want him here, but his reasons for coming were compelling. And, if she was honest, she had to admit she would have done the same. He was half out of his mind with worry for the little girl and his friends, and she was heckling him.

The urge to apologize nagged at her. But apologies to this man came harder than most, so she simply sidestepped the issue by turning from him. She was still busying herself with the care of the stallion when he walked away.

"Do we risk a fire?" Rafe tossed down an armful of wood gathered as he returned from tethering his mount in the shade of an aspen.

In the waning afternoon the temperature hovered between hot and hot as hell, but nightfall would bring drastic change. At this altitude and season they would be in no danger of freezing, but they would pass an uncomfortable night denied the warmth of fire.

Driving a needle through a length of leather, Valentina finished the minor repair of a bridle before she replied. "There's no reason we shouldn't, and every reason we should."

Succinct, implicit, and he understood. "You still think we're being watched, and a cold camp would be suspicious?"

"My gut feeling is there's no one out there. From what we learned of the Apostles, its clear they're smug and arrogant. The type who believe they're infallible by divine right and, by that right, destined to strike fear in the influential and the mighty."

"Paralyzing fear."

"Exactly. And because it wouldn't occur to them that Pat-ck McCallum would dare go against their demands and con-itions, we have a certain degree of liberty."

"For a while, until we're closer to the cabin," Rafe inter-reted. "If you're guessing right."

"*If.* There's always one." Laying the bridle aside, she re-urned the needle to a small kit and snapped it shut. "In any ase, precaution is always sensible. So, to avoid suspicion, we ct natural, do as casual wanderers of the desert would."

"Make camp for the night, build a fire, cook a meal," he dded to the list.

"A quick bath in the stream." She was rising from the stone aat served as her seat. "Before the temperature drops."

"I'll gather more wood and start the fire," Rafe volun-ered. "When you've finished, I'll take a dip, as well."

"Right." A glance at the sky told Valentina they hadn't ong before the sun slipped behind a mountain and the tem-erature slide began. Stepping to her saddlebags, she took out towel and soap and a change of clothes. "I won't be long." Iesitating, she added, "Leave the meal to me. If you insist aat we travel together, we might as well be fair in the division f chores."

"Sure." With his agreement Rafe let the matter drop.

He was gathering wood from a deadfall, keeping a cautious ye for rattlesnakes, when she crossed the clearing to the edge f the stream. There was a startled instant when he wondered ' she planned to bathe within view. As she followed the curve f the tumbling stream until she was beyond his sight, he was ncertain if he was pleased or disappointed. Refusing to dwell n this strange reaction to a woman who was everything he ound distasteful, he let the quest for fuel take him in an op-osite direction.

Fire blazed in a stone lined pit, and coffee steamed over a mall iron grill, when she reappeared.

"Better?" With casual nonchalance he fed another broken mb to the flames.

"Much." Crouching by the fire across from him, she let its eat dry her hair. "There's a small pool beyond the first bend. Iot deep or wide enough for a swim, but perfect for a bath.

A cold one.'' The warning was a peace offering as she grate
fully accepted a cup of coffee. ''Much colder than I ex
pected.''

''The stream must come straight out of the mountain, the
moves too quickly through the canyon to catch the heat of th
day.'' Heavy with resin, the last limb he tossed into the p
sent up a shower of sparks as it smoldered and seethed befor
erupting into flames.

Valentina leaned against a boulder, folding her hands abou
the cup. A small smile played over her lips. ''Having secon
thoughts?''

''Not about the bath.''

He rose from his place as she regarded him steadily ove
the rim of the tin cup. ''About me, then? About whether o
not I can do what Simon and Patrick McCallum want fron
me?''

''About whether anyone can do what Simon expects an
Patrick needs.'' Tossing the last of his coffee onto the fire
Rafe watched it dance and sizzle and rise in steam, as the cu
fell from lax fingers. His eyes were dark and shadowed whe
his gaze met hers. ''Can anyone save Courtney?''

Saying no more, he left the fire. While he gathered clothin
and supplies for his bath, she saw the weight of the burden h
carried. If she failed, he would see it as his failure, as well. I
he returned to his friend empty handed, without the child wh
had been given to him at birth to protect, it could destroy him

Her concern for his intrusion remained constant, her nee
to work alone never lessened, but anger vanished. She wante
to save this child. Dear God! She wanted to save them all. A
she'd wanted to save the one she'd failed. Blinking back sud
den pain, she turned her gaze to the fire, surrendering to damn
ing memories of fateful hesitation and loss.

''Not this time.'' She roused and muttered only to hersel
''Not again.''

Desperate words drifted away, lost in the crackle of fire
The past became the present, and seconds hours as she sa
held captive by the flames, yet hardly seeing them. She wasn'
sure what drew her from her mesmerized distraction. Perhap
it was a sound, or a thought. Or a need.

''Rafe.''

He stopped at the water's edge, but didn't face her.

"If there's any way, any at all, I'll give back Jordana and Patrick's little girl." *But first I'll give her to you.* A promise made, but left unspoken. "I'll do my best, I give you my word."

"If!" The word was a snarl, softly savage. "As you said, there's always the qualification. Every bet hedged. Always the little doubt, the hesitation."

Valentina's face crumpled, her eyes grew somber. She'd wanted to give him some small measure of hope, instead she'd intensified his wariness and mistrust. Regret turned her voice distant. "Yes." Her tone grew colder, more aloof, as she dealt with her failure. "Always."

Drawn by something in her tone, something beneath the coldness, Rafe turned to look at her, seeking to understand the sound of unresolved pain. But her attention had returned to the fire, her head down, her face half-hidden by the gleaming curtain of her hair. The sky at her back etched the rim of the canyon in vermilion. A color so vivid the flames she found mesmerizing paled and faded, reminding that darkness followed light. Then would come the cold.

The sun rode the rim, sending shafts of light glancing over stone. The stream splashed and burbled, beckoning in a misty rainbow. And Valentina O'Hara stared into the fire.

He watched her, so still, so silent, wondering, as before, how she'd come to be one of Simon's Marauders. Vowing, once more, that one day he would know, he followed the path that beckoned.

Their meal was finished. Plates and pans had been scrubbed with sand, rinsed in the stream and put away. Only the coffeepot steamed over the fire, a fragrant vapor blending with the lingering scent of bacon and beans. Range fare, the cowboy's lot. Quick, no-nonsense, plentiful and filling.

The fire burned down, sending little spurts of flame flicking from white-hot embers. Rafe would add more wood later. Large, green logs to smolder, then burn, then smolder again through the night.

Beyond the circle of their camp the canyon was silent. Its

stillness broken only now and again by the stealthy scuttle o nocturnal creatures. A summer moon sailed the sky. A perfec golden globe with a great rough face seeming so near one nee only lift a hand to touch it. Leaves of the aspen shivered an quaked in the riffling breeze. Their green and gold dress, harbinger of autumn, made more golden by the light of th moon.

A log crumbled into ash. A display of sparks and flam painted fleeting silhouettes and shadows over the tumble o stones marking the boundary of their camp. In that transien moment, Valentina's image was sketched in red rock, sombe and still. As silent as the night.

Like the night, her silence was brooding, not sullen. Pen sive, not reproving. She had accepted him as another of th inescapable burdens of this brief measure of her life. As on who traversed this part of the world must accept the threat o rock slide, or rattlesnake, and cactus spine. And in the pensiv brooding lurked the curious air of sadness he'd sensed beneath the arrogant assurance.

With his gloved hand, he lifted the pot from the grill, judg ing from the heft of it that only one cup remained. One thick thoroughly boiled, concentrated cup. Holding the pot poise over the fire, he spoke softly. "More?"

Responding vaguely, she looked at him through eye blinded by her thoughts, not by fire.

"More coffee?" he offered again. "One cup left."

Her brows arched down in concentration, as if she couldn' draw her mind from its preoccupation. "One?"

"If you dare." A deliberate move splashed liquid agains tin in a hollow rattle and a billow of bitter steam. "The devil' own brew, by now."

"Coffee?"

"If you wish to call it that."

She moved her head in refusal. "No, thanks."

Rafe smiled, but only with his lips, as he watched her "Wise choice."

"I haven't always made them."

Hesitating in the act of rising, Rafe knelt on one knee. "A common human failing."

"To those for whom failure is an option." Her gaze settled again on the fire, avoiding his.

Rafe's look swept over her, his scrutiny long and hard. "But not an option for you."

Valentina nodded her agreement.

"And not this time."

She was unresponsive for so long he thought she wouldn't answer. When she did, it was no more than a word, born on a breath slowly exhaled. "No."

Climbing to his feet, he waited for more. When there was nothing, he moved to the stream to rinse the pot, readying it for the morning and the last time. The next night's camp would be cold and dry, after a longer day on a trail even more grueling. Over the simple fare of dinner, she'd given this terse explanation for a short, acclimatizing first day. And in her tone there had been no hint of mercy for man or beast, or woman, in the trek ahead.

Mercy was the last thing Rafe expected, and far from his thoughts when he knelt by the stream. As he rinsed away the dregs, fallen leaves drifted by in the froth of icy water, brilliant and beautiful in the light of the moon. But he had no time for beauty as he lifted his eyes to the mountains.

Courtney was there, trapped in a squalid shack with a madman.

So far away. So far yet to go. So little time.

And only one hope.

Valentina.

She was laying out her bedroll when he returned from the stream. In base camp he'd noted an orderliness about her, with a place for everything, and everything in its place. He saw it now, even in the wilderness. Perhaps especially in the wilderness.

He wondered, not for the first time, how much of it was her nature, how much her training. One schooled by the commander of The Black Watch would never be caught off guard, never unprepared.

"Turning in?" A rhetorical question, given the obvious, but he made no apology as he tended the fire.

"We'll be making an early start in the morning. At first

light." She looked up from her chore. "If you're determined to go on."

"I'll be ready. First light."

In the blink of an eye something changed in a subtle altering of her expression. He thought at first it was a small nuance of relief, but when she turned briskly back to making her bed, he knew he was mistaken. He'd seen only the changing of light, a softening of her features created by the flattering glow of the fire.

"Pity," he muttered, not certain why, then covered the sound with his own preparations for the night. He worked first with the fire, making it ready for the duration. Next was his bedroll, spread across from hers by the pit. And, as was his nature, there was a place for everything. A panther from the bayous would no more be caught unprepared or unguarded than one of The Black Watch. While he worked, according to his nature and by habit, his thoughts were of Valentina.

She'd come, accepting the burden of the impossible. There would have been no other choice for her had she been given one. But there were others who had done the same with more humanity.

Cold. With quick glancing looks, he watched her, judging her as she moved with meticulous care, emotionally uninvolved, never concerned that a child was out there. A tiny girl, frightened and in danger, was business to her. An assignment, a job to be done, no more, no less. He questioned neither her ability nor her will to succeed. Only her compassion.

"An assignment, that's all that matters. Not that it's a child." Anger surged black and corrosive as he slammed the pot on a stone by the fire. "Not that it's Courtney."

For all he knew he could have been shouting. But when he found her looking at him, a puzzled look on her face, he knew his furious words had been an unintelligible growl. She hadn't heard, hadn't understood.

"It's nothing," he snapped with strained patience when she continued to stare. Surging to his feet, needing to distance himself from her, with a brusque gesture he parried her concern. "Go on with what you were doing. I've a few things to see to before I bed down El Mirlo and then myself."

"The horse is fine." Her eyes were narrowed, her gaze still questioning. "I saw to him and Black Jack a bit ago."

"The gelding allows very few people near him."

"He let me." There was no challenge nor arrogance in her tone. A simple statement of truth.

"I should have realized he would." Rafe had begun to realize she shared a kinship with animals that verged on magical. He'd seen the first suggestion of her skill in the corral and the charming of Black Jack. Then more on the trail as the horse responded to her touch and her voice, taxing equine strength in answer.

She shared an astonishing rapport with the horse. Yet with the human animal she kept herself apart, feeling and caring little.

"He's set for the night, but a familiar face in a strange place wouldn't hurt." She offered the excuse, perceiving Rafe's need to get away. "Nor would a bit of praise from the one he's tried most to please."

"You think so, do you?" Rafe's comment was as caustic as his mood. His face was a cynical mask in the weaving play of firelight.

Valentina sat back on her heels, her knees in the dust. With her fingers linked before her, there was a calm about her as she faced the brunt of his contempt. "An observation and a suggestion." A slight shrug, and a tendril broke free of the orderly cascade of her hair. Swaying against the smooth line of her throat, it was silky and darkly fascinating in the absence of the many hues drawn from it by the sun. "My apologies, no interference intended, I assure you."

He had no answer for his mood, no plausible excuse, no apologies of his own. And no inclination to accept her assurance or those she offered. "I'll see to the horse."

Stalking into the shrouding darkness, he wondered what the hell that little skirmish was all about. Why had a simple suggestion sent him into a rage and an apology made it worse? Was it simply that he didn't like her?

No. Like or dislike had nothing to do with it. He'd learned long ago in his years with McCallum American, then McCallum International, that liking was never a prerequisite for working successfully with one or dozens of people.

Then why, he wondered again, and was no closer to an answer when El Mirlo lifted his head, whinnying a soft greeting.

Much later, having deliberately whiled away more time than any duty or communion with his horse required, he found the camp quiet and as he'd left it. The fire burned low in a bed of embers that would ward off the chill of the small hours. The coffeepot waited for the morning. With her saddle for a pillow, his traveling companion slept the sleep of an untroubled mind.

"Worry." The hoarse command was hardly a ripple in the calm of the camp as he scowled at her over the pale blush of the fire. "Toss. Turn. Feel. Care! Damn you, care!"

He wanted to shake her, make her hear and heed him. And he knew then he had the answer to his mood. He wanted her to feel, to become involved, to understand the desperation and face what she must do with more than dispassion. Rafe understood that she must be cool and poised, undeterred by clouding emotions. But he knew, as well, that she must care.

Courtney needed for her to care.

Rafe Courtenay needed for her to care.

Drawing a harsh breath, he shook his head wearily. He couldn't in a million years explain to himself, any more than he could to anyone else, why he felt so strongly that caring would be the key to survival. Yet, even as he lacked the words, he was convinced that when she was balanced on that fine line between success and failure, caring could and would tip the scales in Courtney's favor.

Was it simply that? That it was the extra dimension that made the impossible possible? Or was it more?

"Caring." The word rang hollowly through the imperturbable peace of the canyon. With the echo of it resounding in his mind, and keenly conscious of every worn and tortured muscle, he stretched out on his bedroll. He would not bother with taking off more than his hat, for he would not sleep.

Not tonight, nor any night, until Patrick's child was safe.

Lying with his head leant against his saddle, arms folded at the back of his neck, he stared at the sky and thought of the woman who slept within a touch of his fingertips. He puzzled over her, worried about her, and struggled to find the key to understanding. Perhaps then he could replace enmity with empathy, though he knew it was the last thing she would want from him.

Tracing patterns and paths of stars, as the world spun on its path through the night, he let himself drift. He had no idea how long he'd lain there—an hour, two, most of the night.

Perhaps it could have been nearly morning when he heard it—the sound. A ragged, nearly silent cry that made his blood run like icy sludge through his veins, and shivers scratched with ghostly claws at his spine.

There was a desperateness in the cry, and for all its softness, raw, bleeding anguish. In a frozen moment of sheer disbelief, mistrusting his perceptions, he wondered if he'd drifted into a somnolent trance, with this part of a waking dream.

But when he heard again the whispered lament, its pain telepathic, inescapable, he knew there was no dream. The cry of hidden grief torn from the unguarded mind of sleep was as real as life, as hopeless as death. And there was more as he lay listening, hearing when he didn't want to hear. More than he could bear.

Valentina O'Hara was in agony. Private, secret agony. Heart-shattering, soul-destroying agony.

"No!" Denial rang clearly through her garbled mutterings. Harsher, stronger, as if she fought back an overwhelming tide. In that he was glad, for he wanted no more.

"I can't," she whispered again.

He stiffened, dreading.

"Oh, God! Please."

Rafe knew then there would be more. And worse. Heart laboring, body clenched, he waited. A wait that would not be long.

"No-o-o." She turned, tossing, twisting in her bedroll, trying to escape her own thoughts, her own mind. "Don't! Don't let it be. Please."

Mournful plea descended to sobbing hopelessness. Cursing, Rafe bolted from his bed, scarcely aware of chilling sweat flooding like rivulets of heart's blood down his chest. If the first was anguish, this was far more, far worse. He was witnessing a soul's descent into hell.

Kicking away the light blanket he'd added to his bedroll,

he skirted the edge of the pit. Kneeling at her side with no idea what he should do, he touched her forehead cautiously, half expecting he would find her burning with fever. Instead she was cold, her skin clammy, as she cringed from his touch.

"Valentina." As he whispered he stroked her brow, seeking to quiet her troubled thoughts. Her eyes were open, dark with pain. The unseeing stare of a sleepwalker who walked only in the horror of her mind. "Shhh, Irish," he murmured, and then again, as she quieted at the sound of his voice, "Shhh."

The hand that clamped over his wrist was strong, stronger than it would ever be beyond the dream. "David?"

"No." He brushed her hair from her face. "Not David."

"I'm sorry."

"I know."

"Sorry. So sorry."

"He knows."

"I couldn't." Her body writhed. "I tried. I really tried."

Rafe had never heard such desolation. Nothing had ever torn at his heart as completely. When he took her in his arms, cradling her body in the curve of his, he wondered if it was himself he comforted in his helplessness or Valentina in her grief.

She was restive in his embrace. Every muscle taut, vibrating with tension. He spoke to her softly, a singsong of sense and nonsense. He stroked her lightly, as he did Patrick's little ones when they were hurt and afraid. Degree by tiny degree she relaxed. So imperceptibly he was hardly aware until she sank deeper and more pliantly into his arms.

Holding her, he rocked instinctively, the gentle, rhythmic motion that had forever comforted the hurt. She stirred only once, muttering, denying herself even this small solace. "No."

"Shh. You're all right." He countered her resistance, his grasp supporting, but unconfining. "I'll keep you safe."

"David?" Her fingers clasped at the collar of his shirt, seeking a lifeline in chaos. "I'm sorry."

"He knows." Rafe was sure that he did. As he was sure David was dead and Valentina blamed herself. "Wherever he is, David knows."

Time became his ally, and with its passage the horror diminished. When she was quiet and at peace at last, he left her tucked warmly in her blanket and his own.

When morning came, she wouldn't remember. Rafe Courtenay would never forget.

He'd wanted her to feel, to care. He'd learned that she did. Deeply, passionately. More than anyone he'd ever known. But he'd learned something of himself as he'd listened to her tortured whispers in the dark.

He'd discovered that he cared. More than was reasonable. More than he wished.

For Valentina O'Hara.

Five

A harness jangled, a horse whickered in the darkness. Both quieted by the touch of a steady hand.

"Ho, boy. Easy now." Valentina's voice carried softly through the barely fading gloom as Rafe looked up from his own tasks to watch. She moved deftly, the inborn skill lending to every gesture the illusion of slow motion. Without appearing to hurry, she accomplished a great deal effectively, precisely. Before the first ray of the sun shot over the rim of the canyon she had finished. By the time the second shaft of light beamed down on the canyon floor, she was mounted.

Swinging into the saddle, Rafe cast one last look over what had been their campsite. Only the most unrelenting observer would find signs of this interval in their journey. The fire had been smothered, the pit refilled and covered with branches from the deadfall. Supplies they no longer needed were stored within a crevice in a small landslide to be retrieved another time.

They traveled light out of necessity, with the trail ahead promising an incredible challenge. By day's end the way would be too steep. Impossible for these best of mountain horses, yet only difficult for an experienced climber. From the dossier given him by Jim, in turn supplied by Simon, Rafe knew Valentina had done some rock climbing. As she'd done some of a number of things.

"Busy lady," he muttered as he turned in his creaking saddle to find her watching him. Beyond a mumbled good morning over a cup of coffee, she hadn't spoken. Dispatching it quickly, she'd rolled to her feet, stood by the fire as if storing heat against the chill of dawn, then walked away to perform whatever morning rituals she observed, leaving him to his.

They'd met again by the horses, two shadows moving silently in muted darkness. With the coming of the sun, he saw she was dressed as she'd dressed before, jeans, boots, Stetson. A shirt of the same practical style, only differing in tint. The day before she'd worn white, the light color better to repel the heat. Now she wore pale blue, which, in the backlit radiance of dawn, made her skin seem dusky in contrast. A third shirt he'd glimpsed in her pack was ruddy brown, of a coarser, thicker material. The color the hue of the rocks. Camouflage. Protective coloration to guard against the chance of discovery. The sturdy fabric to guard against the rigors of their climb.

"Wise."

"Talking to yourself Mr. Courtenay?" A tightening of the reins quelled Black Jack's eager response to her voice.

"Thinking aloud."

"About what lies ahead?"

"Maybe."

"You can still turn back. If this should go wrong…" She stopped, reluctant to address the consequences of failure. When she spoke again her voice was low, more thoughtful than he'd ever heard it. "You needn't put yourself through this."

"Don't I?" El Mirlo stamped and snorted, as impatient to be moving as Black Jack.

"Simon says Patrick McCallum is an exacting man." Quietly she amended, "He says, as well, that there's no man fairer nor more compassionate. If you go back now, he wouldn't blame you."

"I would." Rafe's retort was succinct, final. Wheeling El Mirlo about, he turned his bleak gaze to the mountain, then to Valentina. He stared at her through the gloom, seeing little evidence of her tumultuous slumber and no glimmer of memory. He could almost believe the night had been the dream he'd thought it—were it not for the half-moon brand of her nails on his wrist. Were he not an obdurate realist he might convince himself he hadn't held her in his arms, if the soft heat of her body and the fragrance of her hair did not linger in his mind.

He didn't presume to know the import of the night or its heartache. David was only a name called in the throes of despairing grief, a name linked with catastrophic circumstance. Beyond that Rafe knew nothing of this David who lived in a nightmare, neither who he was nor what he'd been to Valentina. Nor why Rafe Courtenay should care.

An impatient jerk of his head and a silent curse banished the errant recollection. He would not risk the distraction. He could think of nothing but taking Courtney from the brutal hands that held her. Complete concentration must be centered on this day. Second of three desperately precious days.

"It's time, Irish." He said the name softly. The name that had summoned her from the hell and horror of a dream. "Do you lead? Or shall I?"

"I lead, it's my job, my responsibility." Valentina had sensed a difference in him, but as she touched a spur to Black Jack, in a fleeting glimpse she saw the familiar unyielding austerity in his face. Startled that it should matter, to assure herself that it didn't, she called over her shoulder, "Stay close. Fall behind and I'll leave you. Get lost and you're on your own."

"Just do your job, Miss O'Hara, and don't bother looking back. I promise you I'll never be more than a step behind." There was no sign that she heard, and Rafe said no more as he guided his mount in Black Jack's path.

His trust was not misplaced in the hours to come. The gelding lived up to his reputation, scrambling, lunging, dodging, with canny instinct, stones that tumbled into his path. Ever pursuing the stallion, trampling in his tracks even as dust crumbled from the sharp-edged fault left by pounding hooves.

The day was timeless. One hour slipped into another with only the sound of their passage and the scurrying flight of animals breaking the silence. When she called a halt in a clearing at the base of a butte, though there was daylight for yet another hour or more of riding, Rafe made no objection. The horses were done.

Valentina dismounted, unsaddled Black Jack and left him ground-tied to forage through the brush. It took her only minutes to find the tank, a small holding of water trapped in a worn depression of tall stone. A life-giving phenomenon of this land. Though she'd never been this way before, she knew it existed, as those who had briefed her promised. Tanks, or tanques, were marked in minds and memories, rather than on maps. Only word of mouth and honor guided the unfamiliar high desert traveler.

Crouching by the oval worn in stone over time and serving now as keeper of its small store of treasured liquid, she let her gaze wander to Rafe. He'd done as he promised, keeping up, keeping quiet. He knew the country well in general, if not this particular trail. He knew its exigencies and its quirks. He understood its demand on human wayfarers and conducted himself in accord. In harmony with the land, not against it.

A surprising circumstance, when she let herself think of it. An extraordinary man, a ruggedly handsome man, if she would let herself admit it.

Refusing the intruding thoughts, she shifted her attention to the terrain and the site of their final camp before they reached the rimland. As the land they'd left behind, it was barren, stark, with a ghostly beauty. Yet it was more. More barren, more stark. In inexorable beauty, more dramatic. More deadly.

A land in which water was rare and yet its master sculptor, its demon, its gift. Today there was only the small tank and red dust. Other days, with a swift gathering of clouds unleashing violent and sudden torrents on the earth, flash floods could come roaring from mountain and through deep canyon. Water most savage, bringing with it a surge of trees and boulders, turning dust to silt, and peace to death and chaos.

Some days, but not this day. The pristine sky was clear and calm. No great wind snaked through the canyon, whipping trees and shrubs or toppling stone. The air did not bear that prickling, electric prophesy of storm. There was no respite, good or bad, from the sun.

Laying her hat aside, she scooped a palmful of water from the tank. Touching her tongue to it she found it brackish, but not bitter, and no danger to them. With a satisfied nod, she sluiced the palmful over her face and neck, reveling in the transient cool.

A shadow fell before her. Longer, leaner, an embellished replication of Rafe, cast over stone. She didn't look away from it as she spoke. "We'll camp closer to the rim, but refill our canteens here before the horses drink."

Though she couldn't see, as before on the trail, Rafe nodded his agreement.

"When the day cools and the sun sets, the animals will come to drink. By the rim we won't obstruct their way." Valentina realized she instructed him as if he were a tenderfoot. Something that couldn't be further from reality. She was discovering Rafe Courtenay was an unusual mix. A man as at ease in the wild as the conference table, and much like her brothers.

"I assume tonight will be a cold camp." Rafe's voice was rusty from trail dust and disuse.

"The chances that we would be seen are slim to none, but for the sake of caution…"

"A cold camp," Rafe finished for her. Once again admiration for her insight and her skill outweighed a faltering antipathy.

Valentina looked up at him, not as tall as the shadow he cast, not as dark, but far more handsome. Far too handsome, with eyes that seemed to see into her. Fighting back a defensive shiver, she took her hat from the stone to tilt it low over her face as she rose. "We've some time yet before nightfall, I suggest each of us puts it to good use."

She was facing him, their gazes level, for once without challenge. "If Jim's memory serves, there's a small cul-de-sac that will make a temporary corral for Black Jack and El Mirlo. There should be another tank and grass." An absent gesture skimmed back tendrils escaped from the heavy coil that she'd pinned to her crown and covered with the Stetson many hours before. "Enough water and grazing for two horses for a couple or three days. By then someone should have come for them."

There was no need to add that in little more than a day the

hostage situation would be ended. For better or worse, for all of them.

As she moved away, crossing over rock and down incline as if she had not been in the saddle interminably, she was aware again of Rafe following closely. She was aware, as well, that she had grown comfortable and even grateful for that. Unusual for a woman such as she, with a profession such as hers. Once again she related this uncommon trust to his similarity to her brothers. The only men she trusted other than her father and Simon.

And David.

But she couldn't think of him. Thoughts of David opened the door to failure. "I can't fail," she whispered in labored breaths as she skidded down the last incline to the clearing where Black Jack was tethered. "I can't," she said again. "Not this time."

The stallion whickered and nibbled at her sleeve as she caught up his reins. "It's the long way around for you, fella. But after what you've done today, the rest of the way should be a snap. Then it's a day or so of rest and grazing for you."

Black Jack whickered again and shook his head.

"Sorry, fella, not this time." She stroked the long, handsome nose, the powerful neck. "You think you're a mountain goat, but you're far too splendid for that, so this is the end of the trail for you."

The jingle of a bridle and the eager tramping of the gelding's hooves signaled El Mirlo's greeting to Rafe. The man moved silently, swiftly, like a tracker, a hunter. Like Tynan.

"Do you always do that?" Rafe was a pace away, reins in hand, listening, watching.

Because he had been so silent, speaking so rarely, his question was unexpected. Stopping in mid-motion, her fingers tangling in the blue-black mane, she glanced over Black Jack's back at him. "Do I always do what?"

"Do you always talk to horses," Rafe explained. "Or only this one?"

Valentina had no answer. He questioned something she hadn't considered. Something she did without thinking. After a moment, with a lift of her shoulders, she asked, "Doesn't everyone?"

"No, not everyone," Rafe said thoughtfully. "At least, not with the same result." With a cock of his head, he looked from Valentina to Black Jack and back again. "This half-wild beast would walk through fire without a blindfold, if you asked."

"Maybe." She hedged. "And maybe it's simply that he likes the tone and cadence of my voice."

"Maybe." Even as he agreed, Rafe knew it was more than tone and cadence, more than her voice. It was the rare kinship some few shared with the wild beasts. He'd seen it at the base camp. He saw it on the trail as a horse offered up a great heart at her bidding. He saw it now. The human tip of an iceberg and the one saving grace of an aloof and rigid warrior? Or another facet of the tormented woman he'd glimpsed in the dark? A woman who cared too deeply, and hurt so badly she kept her emotions under lock and key. Who appeared to have no recall of shattered locks and broken dreams whispered poignantly as he'd held her in his arms.

"I would doubt it's that simple." Then speaking of locks and broken dreams, he muttered, "But is such ever simple?"

With a curious glance at his bemused countenance, Valentina dismissed the subject for surer ground. "In any case, we haven't the time to make sense out of nonsense. We've plenty of daylight left, but we've plenty to do as well. By the time we water and tend the horse, then construct a corral, we should both be ready for a quick bite and an early bedtime."

"You plan an early start tomorrow?"

"As soon as it's safe to climb. We haven't far to go, but it will be precarious, and I'd like to be in place before midmorning."

She'd had little sleep, and that had been unsettled. Rafe questioned how much more she could do. How steady could her hand be, how true her aim, when the time came? "Rough day tomorrow."

"The roughest," she agreed. "But the shortest."

"Then we should make quick work of the rest of this one." Gathering the reins tighter, Rafe turned El Mirlo toward the path that would skirt the detritus of an ancient avalanche, the path to the second tank.

For once, he led the way, guiding his mount past the fallen

rock and rubble before leaving the gelding to drink. When both horses had drunk their fill, and the clinging mementos of the trail had been curried away, he was first to begin cutting and gathering limbs and brush for a makeshift fence.

He labored relentlessly, shouldering more than his share of the task. Taking from her what he could, leaving her to brace and hold when an extra pair of hands speeded his effort along. In response to her protest he told her firmly that she had not come to build fences. That would be his job. Hers was of more import, and her strength must be husbanded to that end.

Valentina could offer no disputing argument, but neither did she cease her own labors.

The sun was barely above the rim of the canyon when the corral was finished and the horses turned into it. Free of his tether, Black Jack galloped and pranced and explored, testing each boundary, finding cliff walls on three sides, and Rafe's tripod-fashioned fence on the fourth. El Mirlo was only a little less curious as he snuffled at the tank and then the grass, trotting from clump to clump.

"He's magnificent." Valentina leaned an arm against the fence as she watched the gelding with ebony coat shining in the bright edge of twilight, mane flying over an arched neck, tail streaming. "Who would geld such a creature?"

"A fool who didn't know what he had in the colt." Rafe rested his forearms on the fence, his shoulders brushing hers. "In fact, he was only days away from being destroyed when Martin found him and called Patrick."

"Martin?"

"Martin Tyree. The Anglo name given to the old Indian who manages Patrick's stable."

"Given?" Valentina turned her gaze from El Mirlo, letting it rest levelly on Rafe.

"After Martin Luther. Martin is from a time when certain religious factions took it upon themselves to civilize a nation they considered savages. These well-meaning, but totally insensitive people took him and other boys like him from their homes, set them down in another culture with no regard for their own. Cut their hair like white boys, dressed them like white boys and gave them names of religious or biblical figures to replace what they considered unpronounceable anathema of savages. With that they considered their duty done. A smattering of education and the name were all Martin reaped from their efforts before he ran away.''

"History repeats itself," Valentina mused. "A child is taken by those who espouse their own twisted sort of religion."

"Twisted and deadly." The terse response closed the door to any other conversation. For a while they watched the horses in the red glow of the setting sun. Then, as if by unspoken agreement, they turned, walking together to their cold camp.

The evening meal was a spartan affair of water and packaged food. As each leaned against facing boulders, a hush lay between them. A natural void, marking boundaries and personal space as a campfire had the night before. Silence, neither strained nor uncomfortable, reflecting concerns not of this time, not of this place, not of each other.

It loomed before them. The morning. The summit. Courtney McCallum.

Draining the last water from her cup, Valentina set it aside to be stowed and left behind. For the rest of the way, her canteen would be strapped to her side. Only the few personal items she needed and a case containing the disassembled rifle would be stored in the backpack she would carry. Out of necessity and meticulous nature, she mentally cataloged every item, mapped every move, leaving nothing to chance. A place for everything, everything in its place—everything within her control.

At last, weary from her thoughts, she tilted her head against the stone. Her hands lay loosely over her bent knees, her lashes drifted down to hover at her cheeks. Through their soft sable veil, her unseeing gaze rested on her companion. In a rare moment of peace, refusing to worry when worry would only lead to more, she let her meditation drift where it would. A small smile eased the grave, tired lines of her face as her brothers marched into her mind. Devlin, Kieran, and Tynan, strong, purposeful men. Each with his own strength, his own purpose. Different, yet so much alike. Each so much like Rafe.

"What are you thinking?" Drawn by her stillness, intrigued

y an uncommon softness easing the strain from features that were really quite lovely, Rafe put his last task aside unfinished.

Rousing reluctantly from this safest of places, the sanctuary of her family, her look was empty and uncomprehending.

"What do you think of?" He asked again in a hoarse half whisper. Driven to ask, but loath, even as he spoke, to disturb he hovering hush of the rim. "Where do you go? What place within you preserves your sanity on such nights as this? What gives you that look of accord? Who?"

As he waited, Rafe, who was never impatient, was strangely impatient. Deep in his heart he wondered if the answer was David. Was it he who brought stillness and serenity on the white charger of day, and horror on the maddened mare of darkness?

David. She'd called his name in the black void of night. Would she now?

"What, Valentina?" There was vital need in the repetition that Rafe couldn't define. "Who?"

"My family. Tonight, my brothers," she answered quickly. Too quickly, and found she could barely restrain herself from adding...*you.*

"Devlin, Kieran, Tynan." He supplied names from the dossier. In saying them something tense and binding unraveled in his chest. "Unusual names."

"Irish."

Rafe nodded and remembered again that it suited her to be Irish. That it suited him that she was Irish. "What sort of men are the brothers of Valentina O'Hara? Tell me about them."

"There isn't a lot to tell."

"Somehow I doubt that."

Shrugging away his dissent, she insisted mildly, "They're good, but ordinary, men."

"Ordinary by O'Hara standards, but, I would venture, by no others."

Slanting a weary look at him, she speculated, "The dossier."

Thumb and forefinger slipped his Stetson back a notch as he nodded.

"Did you memorize the damn thing?"

"Yes." Unequivocal, no hedging the truth.

"Yes?" Her look turned incredulous. "Why? What earthly purpose would that serve?"

Unperturbed by her demand, or the creeping sarcasm in it, he smiled, and in the dim light his face was transformed. "Just accept that it's the way I conduct myself, and humor me."

"Humor you? By telling you what you already know?"

Rafe nodded once more. "From your perspective."

"Why?"

It was his turn to shrug with a detachment far from candid. "To pass the time in an evening that promises to pass slowly." The smile flitted over his features again. "And, as I said, to humor me."

She told herself it was not to humor him that she complied. And was as certain that not even his smile and the roguish teasing in it swayed her. It was more, she wanted to believe, that he was right. The distraction of conversation would pass a nerve-wracking evening far more quickly. And what safer subject than her family? "What would you like to know?"

"Everything. Anything. Whatever you would like to tell."

She abandoned the study of her fingers as they moved with a restlessness of their own over the corded seam at the knee of her jeans. "I have a sister. But you know that from the dossier."

"Patience." Rafe did not say that he'd met her sister, briefly. In one of the strange coincidences of an increasingly small world, in the unlikely converging of different circles, the paths of Patience O'Hara and Rafe Courtenay had crossed. For an evening they had talked and shared a meal under the watchful eyes of Matthew Winter Sky.

Matthew, another of Simon's own, Rafe's friend as well as Patrick's. Patience's love and a fortunate man.

After that evening in Patrick's hilltop villa on the outskirts of Sedona, Rafe had never seen her again. But he'd never forgotten her. Patience was younger than her sister, though by less than a year. She was not so quiet, nor so aloof, but the same strength was there. The physical resemblance was strong, even striking. One more explanation for the moment of déjà vu the first time he'd seen Valentina.

"Patience is the steady one of us, the quietest." At his look of askance and surprise, she amended, "At least she was as a kid. I suspect the rest of us are as steady now. Part of growing up. With it, I suppose we've all grown quieter."

"As you are."

Scrubbing her palms over the legs of her jeans, Valentina only then considered the long hours she'd spent with this man, and how little she'd spoken. "Yes."

"Do you have a favorite brother?"

"Choosing one over the other would be impossible. There's something about each of them that..." Valentina shook her head with a ghost of a smile. "I can't explain. I only know that if they weren't my brothers, I'd be in love with all three of them. Tynan for his gentleness, his insight, his empathy and his compassion. Kieran for his orderliness and stubborn conviction that every question has an answer. For his unswerving belief that nothing is impossible and no one is beyond redemption. First and last there's Devlin, the oldest of us and yet the youngest. A rebel among rebels. Our wild one, who challenges life and death every day with a dare and a grin. The one who worries us. The one who makes us laugh.

"These are the individual qualities that come to mind, but, in truth, there's some of each in each. Ty has grinned in the face of life and death. Kieran makes us laugh. And Devlin feels the hurts of others more than his own."

"Quite a family."

"I know."

But who, Rafe wondered, was David? Had he made her laugh? Had he grinned in the face of his own death? Had she been in love with him? Was she still?

"Brothers like yours offer a lot for a man to measure up to."

She nodded, absently, immersed again in private thought.

Rafe knew there would be no more. He'd lost her.

"It's late," she said, stirring at last. "We should turn in."

"In a while." Rafe returned to the small task of taking the spurs from his boots. He wouldn't need them tomorrow.

Valentina sighed as she slid into her bedroll. With her cheek turned into the smooth leather of her saddle, she watched him. As he moved quietly about, she knew she hadn't imagined the change wrought by his smile. In that moment, he could have been Tynan, or Kieran, and even Devlin. In the glimpse of a single smile, she saw much of them in him. He was their sort, with the same toughness tempered by kindness. The same mix of ruggedness and gentleness. The conviction and disbelief in the impossible. The daring, the grin. And, perhaps in a time less grave, the laughter.

The first smile made him more than an austere watchdog. The second made him beautiful—a man like her brothers. And, yes, a man she might have loved long ago, in another time, another place. When she was a woman capable of love.

Long ago, but not now.

She watched him settle back against the stone, the Stetson tilted low over his face. She watched him in his stillness and his quietude, and ached for something she'd lost, yet never had.

"Fool." The condemnation was more breathy sigh than word. And, accepting her lot, yet thinking of his smile, she willed herself to sleep. There were smiles as she tumbled over the gentle precipice, but memories and guilt and David lay in wait in the dark chasm of a dream.

Rafe knew the exact moment she fell. He knew what would come. He knew and he waited, and at the sound of her first whispered cry, he rose. Suffering the unbearable no longer, he went to her and he knelt by her. Brushing back the tumbled mass of her hair, he looked into unseeing eyes and into anguish.

As the moon was rising, casting silver shadows over them, he lifted her in his arms and settled her in his lap. Thus he held her and soothed her, marking the passage of the night by the ever-changing moonscape.

His intention was only to comfort, but even in torment she was sweet, flowing silk in his arms. Her voice was the voice of a temptress, calling to him, needing him, as no woman ever had. The fire in her burned him. And for one mad moment his own need became flame. Searing, torrid desire licked at him, engulfing him.

But only for one moment, and only in fleeting madness, for it was another man's name she called. Another man she needed. And tomorrow, for Valentina, the night would never have been.

"Fool." Her word, but he hadn't understood and didn't know.

His face was bleak, the sardonic countenance of the Creole again. Yet he didn't put her from him, nor cease his soothing. His voice was soft as he spoke, his embrace gentle. Staring over the canyon rim he drew her close, and, though the moon still bathed them in its radiance, the light had gone from the night.

He held her, hearing her whispers in the darkness of his soul. For an eternity he listened. Until the dream ended. Until sleep overtook him. Until there was only tomorrow.

A fly buzzed, sweat trickled into stinging eyes. And little else stirred, neither air nor shrub, nor cloud in the sky. Once, in the uncanny hush, a nearly silent hum and a telltale rasp of undulating scales over parched stone warned of a rattler's disturbed retreat. Valentina did not move.

Dismissing the rigors of the punishing climb, she'd lain for hours, as heedless of the pitiless sun beating down on her. As careless of cruel stone unyielding beneath her slender frame. Her riveted concentration never wavered from the shack—the melancholy testament of the passage of a mad prospector. A travesty of sloth and crumbling stone perched precariously on the sister of their own narrow summit. The one less tall was the bastion of Edmond Brown. Impregnable in concept, if not in strength, for no one could approach it unseen. Neither from the north, the south, east or west.

Above a fringe of weather sculpted juniper and trembling aspen worn like a jeweled necklace, the spire rose in a time and wind scoured pillar of striated sandstone in shades of red and brown. The red-rock of red-rock country. Desolate ground, devoid of brush or boulder to offer secret asylum.

The mad prospector had chosen well. So had the Apostles. Richard Trent's men, deployed since the first day of the kidnapping, could only hover helplessly, in impotent anger, at its base. But on this, the last day, there was hope. Men, women, fathers and brothers, mothers and sisters, too long dormant, awakened from their seething lethargy. The camp, far removed from the main, came alive, stirring with a subdued excitement. No one dared look to the sky and the taller spire. As its shadow marked the crawl of time, they sought only to lure and keep Edmond Brown's concern.

And, as they, Rafe waited. As helpless. As impotent.

She's tired, he thought as he lay only inches from her in their aerie. Tired from the climb, tired from the tension. But none of the exhaustion he perceived was evident in look or manner. He hadn't expected it to be, for this was the purpose of her training. She wouldn't be Simon's best had she not the strength to cope with the physical challenge and mental strain.

But when the ordeal ended, however it ended, what then? Frowning, Rafe hunkered into the cradling crevice of stone, and wondered.

The sun bore down, cloying heat scorching, cleaving the stagnant air. Like a charnel from the past, the stone shack with its one small window loomed across the void. Valentina didn't grow impatient, she didn't stir. The rifle with its powerful scope lay beneath her hand.

As the day crept by, Edmond Brown had been often visible. Always with Courtney at his side. Courtney at his feet. Courtney in his arms. Hostage and shield.

Valentina observed in narrowed contemplation, but never took up her rifle.

When once he would have questioned, now Rafe kept his silence, remembering this was her mission, her shot, her choice. Her conscience.

And in his silence he began to see a pattern. Edmond Brown moved by rote, a creature of habit. Each hour on the hour, the apostle stood at the open door smoking, taking the exact number of deeply drawn inhalations, the same leisurely exhales. Always with the same mocking arrogance. And always with his tiny, unwitting defender near.

Rafe seethed at the conceit. And, though she showed no sign of it, he knew Valentina had recognized the repetitive ritual long before.

While the knowledge calmed him and a growing respect grew more, thirst sawed at his throat. Cramps threatened the long, desiccated muscles, but he lay as still and silent as she. Any move, unseen yet perceived by the visceral sixth sense of the hunted, could betray them. And a child would pay the price of betrayal. A young life too dear to lose for the cost of a sip of water or the ease of a muscle.

There would be no respite as the day, the last day, spun down.

Finally, in the canting light of late afternoon, Valentina stirred, guardedly testing joints and limbs too long immobile. Slowly, the rifle was taken up, the sights checked, the stock set against her shoulder.

With her cheek pressed against the smooth wood, gaze fixed on the door of the shack, she spoke for the first time since ascending the summit. "Time for a smoke. Ten puffs. Not nine, not eleven. Ten, you sanctimonious son of a bitch."

A quarter hour passed, then another. The first hint of evening tinged the sky when the crack of a shot shattered the air. Her mission was finished.

Carefully, woodenly, she laid the rifle aside. Her face was ashen beneath the Stetson's brim, her hollowed eyes blackest blue and haunted. Hands that had been steadier than stone shook before she drew them abruptly into fists. The line of a mouth that had been lovely was hard and grave.

There was no revelry in her expertise. No pride in the exact calculation of distance. No exulting over an exquisitely accurate projection of the physics of trajectory. The shallow curve, the parabolic flight of the bullet was no mystery to her. She'd known by instinct, without conscious thought.

This was her gift and her curse.

As he stared at her, ears still drumming from the percussion, the acrid stench of nitrate filling his lungs, Rafe saw the penalty of gift and curse. Her body shrunken, diminished by more than the privation of water or food, she had withdrawn. Seeking within herself a place of safety and survival in the fragility of an awful moment.

Though time was of the essence, though his heart and soul yearned to be gone from this place, to gather in his arms the child of his friend, his godchild, he was torn by the need to hold the woman. The need to drive away this waking nightmare as he had that which stalked her sleep.

Knowing Richard Trent's men waited only to be deployed, the Creole, man of decisive and unrepentant action, hesitated.

In that precious increment, the decision was taken from him by Valentina.

"Go to her, to Courtney, child of your heart." For all their poetry the words were lifeless. With none of the joy of keeping a vow to give Courtney McCallum back, first to Rafe, who cared so desperately, and then to her family. He was alone, at last. "Pray that she sleeps. If she does, take her carefully and she'll never see, never have to know." A long breath was drawn and held, then released. "And, perhaps, one day she will forget."

Rafe understood, then, the dangerous delay, the twilight shot. This best of Simon's Marauders had come to save more than the life of a child. She had come to save the woman the child would one day become by giving her back unscarred by bloody horror.

He took a step toward this strange and fascinating woman, but she waved him away. The message implicit—*I don't need you. Go to the one who does.*

Standing as she commanded, he let her turn from him. As she stared over the rim, he knew she was truly gone from him, in mind and spirit, as well as in body.

She had spoken for the second time, and the last.

And Courtney waited. Sleeping, God willing, the sweet dreamless sleep of the innocent. As he made ready to begin his descent, he paused for one last glance. There would be no one here if he returned. He knew Valentina would be gone, as surely as he knew that someday he must find her.

This promise he made to himself, and, though she was beyond hearing, he made it to her. "Wherever you go, I'll be there. Believe it or not, accept it or not, Irish, you do need me. You will need me."

With one final look, stored for the days ahead, he slipped over the precipice, beginning the descent in earnest. Finding the way down far less difficult than the climb, he faced an uncommon truth.

For reasons he couldn't explain, Rafe Courtenay, who had never truly needed a woman in his life, needed Valentina O'Hara.

Six

"**W**here is she?"

As his blazing gaze met Simon McKinzie's bland stare, Rafe knew he was a long way and a long while from getting an answer. From long association and experience he knew, as well, there was wisdom in reason when one fenced with the silver haired master of tenacity. Tamping back a surge of anger, he spun about, putting distance and Simon's desk between them.

Striving for vital calm, with shaking fingers curled into his palms in an unconscious sheathing of claws, the panther prowled. Stalking, padding back and forth, a proud and savage creature. The richly paneled walls of this spartan office his cage; beveled glass of arching windows its gleaming bars. And as the veiled and golden light of early evening settled over softly undulating mountains, a man as proud, a friend who meant only to guard those who risked mind and soul and life for The Black Watch, regarded him somberly.

Pausing before a cabinet filled, not with milestones of a long and spectacular career, but mementos of friendships, Rafe felt a momentary cooling of his anger. On crowded shelves lay

works of art, pottery, carvings, bronzes and drawings. Whether
breathtakingly skilled, heartwarming and childish, beautiful or
garish, it made no difference to Simon.

Among them were, per chance, the most telling treasures of
all. A misshapen cigarette lighter fashioned of clay by Simon's
namesake, the young son of Raven Canfield and the first man
recruited for The Black Watch. And, a little apart, standing on
a tiny easel, a miniature watercolor, a seascape. A delicate
masterpiece painted by Ashley Blackmon. Or, more correctly,
Ashley Blakemond. A great, gentle man-child and lost heir.
An extraordinary talent, a life preserved by agents Tanner,
Ryan, and Winter Sky. Three cast in the mold of the best and
the first, David Canfield.

David. The name of dark dreams and whispered horror echoed through his mind in quick suspicion, as quickly silenced.
The Canfields were well and happy, the perfect couple. Vibrant. Dynamic. And Rafe was as certain as he was of anything that no man alive would be Valentina's David.

But that was a mystery to be unraveled, an answer for another time. The answers he needed now only Simon could give
him. Putting speculation and presumption aside, steeling himself to play a waiting game with the master, he immersed
himself in more of these tangible memoirs of Simon Mc-
Kinzie…a clasp of hawk feathers and turquoise, locks of red-
brown hair. A drift of lace winding through a length of
McLachlan plaid. A broken ivory from a piano, the stained
label torn from a bottle of bourbon. A replica of a gold medal.
Trash among treasure, and treasures among trash. Each precious, each with a story. In bits and pieces they were scattered
without rhyme or apparent reason. Unless one knew their sto-
ries.

Some Rafe knew because those few had touched his own
life in some way. Others he did not. And Simon never explained.

But any who saw would understand that in this cabinet were
more than memories. These were the ragtag history of a man
and his work and what mattered to him. Sentiment that would
never find its way into the Washington offices.

Rafe touched the glass that enclosed and protected, leaving

the mark of his fingertip by a rose. Faded and dry, but perfect, a gift from Jordana McCallum.

"How is she?" First to speak in a battle of wills, Simon shattered the still quiet in a rasp of gruff concern.

One small, rare victory for the Creole.

Leaving the cabinet and the rose frozen in time, Rafe did not need to be told Simon spoke of Jordana. His answer was brief, with little joy in victory. "She improves every day."

"She's home?"

"Home, in Sedona." Rafe nodded, giving complete credence to each question, though he was certain Simon knew each answer. "It was Jordana's choice. As soon as she was able our red haired laird would have whisked the whole family away to the safety of his keep in Scotland. She convinced him having Courtney back and none the worse for the ordeal was all any of them needed. She was adamant that staying and dealing with what had happened was better than scurrying away to hide.

"Jordana wins more debates, as she's chosen to call them, with the stubborn Scot than any of the rest of us could ever hope. In this case, as in most, she was right. Staying best." He smiled, a mere tilt of his lips, a softening in his gaze. "Courtney's as bossy and busy as ever. With her daughter, her boys, and Patrick around, Jordana absolutely glows with renewed health and serenity."

"One thing she'll never have to worry over is the Apostles for a New Day." Simon's fisted hand tapped the desk sharply. "Neither she nor anyone else."

Rafe nodded again. He'd read the reports on the disbanding of the group, the separating of false leaders from those innocents who truly believed. "There will be others. Cabals with false prophets, as bad, or worse."

"Vultures." There was sorrow more than distaste in the single word.

"There will always be vultures." Rafe predicted. "But McKinzie and The Watch will always be there to clip their wings."

"So long as there's breath in me." The eyes that could intimidate with a glance reflected the threat of Simon's vow.

"And so long as you have willing and skilled men and woman to aid the cause."

Simon's huge shoulders lifted, not in dismissal, but in deference to the commitment of those whom he had gathered into the unique and clandestine organization he commanded. The Black Watch, a fitting title, recalling the best of warriors among the warring people of Simon's ancestral Scotland. But a misnomer still, as any title would be. Commissioned by a past president, and brought to viable reality by Simon, from the moment of its inception the organization had no recorded name. As those who worked within its sanction had no record of their true objectives.

In the tradition of their leader, they were dedicated men and women, often existing on two levels. One a public life for public interest, intended to comply with the norm. The second, the truest and most consuming, a private life defying any semblance of normality. From the day they became one of Simon's they were a people apart. And from that day must accept that there would be no recorded past, no real present, perhaps no future.

For the cause, for their country and its people, for The Black Watch, and for Simon, their lives were sacrificed. In return, Simon protected them with his.

"We will continue," Simon said at last. "So long as there are those who are willing."

"Willing to do your bidding, no matter the cost to themselves." Rafe hammered home his point without mercy. A point he knew Simon lived with and coped with every day of his life.

The wily Scot's face was blandly expressionless, his formidable body seemingly relaxed. Yet deep in his hooded eyes writhed a veiled emotion few had seen and fewer would believe.

But Rafe saw. Rafe believed. For this was the Simon he knew, the man who cared, perhaps, too much. Even in that knowledge, this was a rare rent in an iron facade. Coupled with his small triumph, this nearly invisible fissure offered as much leverage as he would ever have.

"At all and any cost is true." Rafe spoke softly, and though e asked no question, added even more softly, "Isn't it, Simon?"

"It's true." The words of admission were carefully spaced, a painstaking care that for any but Rafe would have signaled danger.

"Men like David Canfield, nearly destroyed by his partner's death and betrayal." Borrowing an old and familiar habit from Simon, the Creole lifted a hand, folding a finger into his palm as he called the name of each agent of The Black Watch, making each painful, dreadful point. "Jamie McLachlan, concert pianist cum spy, with his shattered hands. Jeb Tanner and a love nearly lost to a serial killer. Mitch Ryan, who can never in all his life save all the children. And Matthew Winter Sky with a portion of his strength lost to a rattler's bite."

With all fingers folded and the fist complete, with a need that transcended a condemning conscience, Rafe went for the jugular. "Now a tortured woman like Valentina O'Hara. A casualty in the line of duty, for The Black Watch. For you, Simon."

"Yes." The snarl of a wounded creature. Simon's guttural accord, whispered on the release of a long-held breath, more compelling than a shout. "Damn you, yes!"

Rafe would not be diverted by the curse spilling out like blood from his wounding thrust. "Yes! Damn me. Damn you. And for what we've asked of her, damn us all!"

The leonine head reared back. With heated currents swirling in their depths, eyes as chilled as a mountain pool stared back at Rafe. A look long and fiercely probing. Discovering a counterpart for his own consuming passion, recognizing the familiar disquiet that left this once invulnerable and unfaltering younger man needful and desperate, Simon, better than any, understood the implacable burden. One that must be resolved, if it meant turning friend to foe.

"Where is she, Simon?"

What he'd seen in Rafe's eyes was in his voice, the sound of compassion. Its depth, more than any threat, became the deciding factor. The quality of singular capitulation.

Leather sighed, the metal structure of the massive chair groaned as tensed muscles relaxed and Simon leaned forward. In a move that was purpose and power controlled, he drew

pen and tablet to him, scrawling in swift, sharp strokes th
address Rafe required. Wondering if this bold challenger un
derstood the driving demand torn from the complexities of hi
own mind and heart, he ripped the sheet from the pad. Foldin
it once, he offered it up with no more fanfare than if it wer
a grocery list.

Taking it from him, Rafe opened the fold of crisp bond
Reading the hard-won lines, with a nod of thanks, he wheele
about.

"Rafe."

The younger man turned again, his hand on the latch. "Yes
sir." In deepening respect born of an uncommon communion
of thought and mind, he waited for Simon to continue.

"Before you go, there's more I have to tell you." Simon':
decisions were never half measures, this would not be
"Things not in any dossier, people and circumstance that laie
the foundation for who she is, if not what." His smile wa:
grave. "A story that won't take long, or much of your time.'

"For Valentina, I have all the time in the world. How coul
I not, Simon?"

"Because of Courtney? And only Courtney?"

Rafe hesitated, a long, slow breath rose and fell in his chest
An uncommon flicker of doubt scored his face. His voice wa:
soberly thoughtful. "I don't know." A shoulder lifted negli
gibly. "It's complicated."

Simon nodded. A truthful answer, the only answer the Cre
ole would ever give. "What I have to say can't resolve you
conflict. But if you understand the life she's lived, the peopl
that made her who she is, if not what...perhaps i
would...ah...ameliorate the situation."

"Perhaps."

Little encouragement, but enough. Tersely, with no frills no
digressions, Simon proffered a concise history of Valentin
O'Hara. In his way of cutting issues to the bare minimum
revealing all that was pertinent, her story was not long. Whe
he finished and fell silent, only one glaring gap remained.

David.

Rafe didn't ask. He understood that David was a story onl
Valentina should tell. If she would. If she could.

"In spite of all I've said, she's fragile. The strongest an

toughest lady I know, but…'' The leader of The Black Watch struggled in this extraordinary breach of his own protocol. Stern lines of frowning indecision threatened the granite composure of his magnificent face as he searched for the right words to make Rafe understand one last important point. ''Precarious…'' His struggle grew no easier. ''Her situation is precarious. It is after each time, but this will be worse. In all her years with The Watch, with all the shots she's taken in the line of duty, she has wounded, but never killed. Until now.''

The steely gaze that had turned inward focused on Rafe. ''Even though she's seen the psychologists and dealt with it, she won't speak of it. Valentina is vulnerable now. Closed in, withdrawn.'' The normally articulate man had come full circle as he muttered, ''Fragile.''

Rafe's dark head inclined in agreement. He couldn't argue with what he'd seen.

''Maybe more fragile than you know.'' The dour Scot drove home his point.

''I came to help in payment of a debt, no more, no less. I won't hurt her, Simon.''

''Are you sure?''

This time a shift of a shoulder, the tilt of his head, signaled Rafe's apprehension. ''As sure as anyone can be.''

''There are other circumstances…''

''I know about David.'' The disclosure was interjected quietly. ''I don't know who he was, or what he was to Valentina, but I know he existed. I know that something tragic occurred, that it involved Valentina and changed her life forever. Until I understand, I give you my word I'll go carefully.''

It was Simon's turn to nod. No more was needed, for there was no one he trusted more than this saturnine man of the bayous. ''Where will you go? Where will you take her?''

With no hesitation or questioning how Simon could guess he would take Valentina anywhere, the answer came quickly. ''To Eden.''

''Patrick's island paradise. His gift to Jordana.''

''Is there a better place to heal a sorrowing soul?''

''No better place for anything,'' Simon avouched. ''The real question is, will she agree to go?''

Rafe smiled then. A smile as mischievous and kind as it

was determined. A smile that changed the line and plane of his face and left one wondering how he ever seemed grim and brooding. The remnants of it lingered as the door swung open. He stood, lean, lithe, gilded in gold against the purple hues of a Blue Ridge sunset. "She'll go."

The latch fell from his hand. With a rakish salute he stepped into twilight. The door closed after him in a decisive click as his footsteps sounded faintly, then faded from the walk.

A hush returned to Simon's mountain retreat, only to erupt into the sudden clamor of an engine gunned to life. The cacophony quieted to a powerful rumble. Halogen lights flicked on, careening off windows, giving the illusion of glancing rays of the sun.

Just as suddenly, all was quiet again in gathering darkness, broken only by the lamp on Simon's desk. Easing his chair around, he stared out the window long after the Jaguar streaked like an ebony thunderbolt from the valley. The last purple ribbon of twilight faded into the shimmering black of the sky, before he moved again. Fumbling absently at a sweater pocket, he searched for the pipe he'd discarded years before.

In the overflow of irritation provoked by a habit long unbroken, the source of his troubled thoughts surfaced. In this sanctum, the only place he called home, surrounded by the mountains he loved, Simon McKinzie wondered what manner of man he'd become.

"A user." Blunt, splayed fingers slapped the arm of the chair. "For malignant cause, without malignant intent."

When he'd first read of Valentina and the sensationalism of her tragedy, he'd looked beyond misfortune and the guilt of failure. Above all, he'd seen a uniquely gifted woman, a superb markswoman, a champion equestrienne. In recruiting her for those skills, he'd hoped to offer her redemption in her own eyes by giving her the chance to do what she couldn't once before.

It was to be a dual-edged bargain—a champion markswoman for The Watch, absolution and peace for Valentina.

A bargain easier made than fulfilled, for the burden of her guilt was deeply entrenched. Absolution was elusive, and without it there could never be the peace Simon wished for her. But he never gave up. With each step she took forward, he gave her more and harder missions, reveling discreetly as she rose to his demands.

But, Simon asked himself, in this case, by breaking his own ironclad rule and revealing personal information, had he gone too far? If there was a chance that what he'd done might bring ease to Valentina, would consequence justify the method?

"Could it?" If what he saw in Rafe Courtenay gave Valentina the peace she needed, would it be worth the worry and the heartache? "Yes!" His fist thumped an armrest. "Every minute of it."

The chair groaned again as he spun back toward the room. Certain now of something the stalwart Creole, himself, did not comprehend, he drew pen and notepad front and center again. Slow, looping strokes turned to flowing lines on paper.

"It was the smile," he groused. Looking down at unconscious thought translated in bold black and mellow cream, the explanation for the deviation from his own inflexible rules leapt out at him. First he chuckled, then he laughed, for the stern and ruthless leader of the most dangerous organization on earth had drawn hearts and flowers.

Laughter boomed. Rich, deep notes erupted again and again in the cavern of his sanctuary. And for the first time in days there was light in the darkness, hope for Simon McKinzie's own redemption.

"Had to be the smile."

A small breeze stirred, rustling the crimsoning leaves of trees along the shore. A fish jumped, slapping water with its tail. Out of the distance, borne on twisting currents of air, came the uneven thrumming of a windlass raising a sail. A loon cried from the marsh. Another answered. The tide lapped in an unchanging rhythm at the weathered pilings of the dock.

Familiar sounds, comforting sounds, all noted subconsciously by rote, out of old habit. Each as natural to Valentina as breathing, each a very real part of her estuarine retreat. She smiled, a wan, sad grimace, but did not stir as the dock swayed beneath her.

The day had grown cold with the passage of time. Her faded

shirt and threadbare jeans offered little protection against its creeping chill. Soon she would be faced with the choice of fetching the sweater that dangled from a jutting piling or returning to the lodge.

Soon, but not quite yet. Not while the boards were still warm at her back and the sun wrapped her in its glowing cocoon.

She had no concept of the time she'd lain there on the splintering, peeling dock. She didn't care. Hours and minutes meant nothing to her as she emptied her mind, drifting with the day, absorbing it, gauging it simply by the rare indulgence of creature comforts.

This haven by the Chesapeake was truly a haven and truly hers. Though the O'Hara estate was only a few miles away by water, and a few more by land, her gregarious family never disturbed her. Who better than the gregarious to understand the need for solitude?

A paradox? No. Simply her family. The O'Haras who were anything but simple.

Stirring, seeking the last bit of warmth from the sun, a real smile, a look of pleasure too rare, flitted over her face. If she had to think, it was best to think of those she loved, and let them keep the rest of the world away.

Time spun away again as they marched through her mind one by one. Not as the rest of the world saw them, or even as she had described them to Rafe Courtenay, but as they were to her. The special people, as she remembered them.

Patience, pretty and sweet, youngest and yet bravest. The small, feminine embodiment of Francis of Assisi. Who ran tiptoe through field and stream, collecting a menagerie of lost and hurt creatures fortunate enough to cross her path.

Tynan, thoughtful, thought provoking family philosopher, who made her think and understand her thoughts. One who believed in the healing power of solitude, and that it needn't be lonely. Who found his own, for reasons of his own, on a Montana ranch.

Kieran, the determined. A child of the modern world with old-fashioned codes. Living proof of a wonderful cliché, a black-haired knight in shining armor in search of dragons to slay. Or, for lack of armor and dragons, a gallant seeking out the challenge of the impossible, making it possible. As only Kieran could.

Lastly, but before them all, the eldest in years, youngest in spirit, Devlin. Laughing, teasing big brother. Guardian and teacher. Hero and thorn in a young sister's existence. Restless wanderer, exuberant adventurer. Risk taker extraordinaire among a family that lived for adventure and thrived on risk. Devlin, with nine lives and the luck of the Irish, always with an edge of mischief and a devilish grin.

And best, Keegan and Mavis, foundation of the O'Hara family. Brilliant, dynamic. Whimsical and wonderful. Strength and guiding force in the formative years of their children, anchor for the adults they became. An uncommon union. An uncommon man, an uncommon woman, a part of whom existed in each of them.

Only their strengths. Our weaknesses are our own.

Valentina never knew if the pain filled admission was spoken or only a thought. There was never the time to know. As quickly and as devastating as a dagger to the heart, as the smile her family could always draw from her faltered, David was there. In her thoughts, in her heart. An oddly nebulous figure, but as she would forever see him. Tall, handsome, beloved, standing with rigid courage in a hostage grip. His captured weapon a deadly threat at his throat, his eyes pleading with her to do what both knew she must. Certain she would not hesitate.

David's eyes, David's face.

But, somehow, not.

The face that looked from the shadow of memory was leaner, darker, older. The piercing gaze of green eyes, not golden brown, speared through the void of despair to the arid desert of her soul. Lips that shaped her name were sterner, cynical. The voice that should have been soundless, yet murmured softly to her, was deep, and rich. Haunting and tormenting with comfort she didn't merit, couldn't accept.

Green eyes. Cold and probing and yet...

Valentina's hands jerked, taut fingers covered her face, denying the blurring of memory. Though the pain was more than she could bear, though she avoided it if she could, she didn't want to forget. She wouldn't. Not David. Not ever.

Succumbing with perverse gratitude to the deluge, bit by brutal bit the past unfolded unhampered in mind and reverie. For once she welcomed it and with it the sorrow.

Waves of guilt and regret washed over her, sweeping away the last shred of disorder. Grief, elemental, without ambivalence, tore at her, body and heart. And with its constance consumed her, excoriated her, sending her lurching, at last, to her feet. Spinning drunkenly, like a dervish courting ecstasy after penance, arms lifted in supplication, she sought some escape.

Escape, but never freedom.

A hoarse cry rose in chorus with the loons, then sank to a ragged whisper. "Never."

Exhausted, she collapsed again on the dock. Knees drawn to her chin, face buried in her arms, she curled into herself. And with her own cry ringing hollowly in her mind, she knew nothing could take away the guilt. A hundred Edmund Browns, a hundred successful rescues, couldn't ease her loss. Nor could a hundred green gazes. A hundred soothing voices.

For Valentina O'Hara, there was not, and must never be, forgiveness.

Tears she thought finished long ago streamed from her eyes, soaked the sleeve of her blouse and turned it dark. She wept for the past, she wept for the future. When the well of tears ran dry, she wept without them for the love that lived only in grief.

Finally quiet, finally calm, she huddled on the dock. Numb, without thought and, for a precious while, unfeeling, she had no idea when the chill crept into her bones and the sound of the engine into her mind. At first, as she became aware of it, she was certain she imagined the subtle nuance, the small rumble. Her little part of shore was isolated, removed from popular lanes of traffic. That she might have visitors never occurred to her. She was home so seldom guests were infrequent and few.

Mercifully distracted, she sat woodenly, listening, concentrating. One moment there was nothing. More the next. And the next.

The deep and heavy thrum grew stronger and unmistakable only the flicker of an eye before a small sloop rounded a bend and hugged the shore. The natural inclination was to expect her family, yet the craft was unfamiliar and distinctively different from the weathered old tub Keegan O'Hara loved. A name painted on the dazzling white of its bow and the logo on pristine sails were indistinguishable from her distance and angle.

A weekend sailor, she concluded. One who had lost his way.

An uncommon occurrence in her little crook of the estuary, but never the bay. Curiously, she welcomed the temporary intrusion. Anything and anyone would be welcome. Any diversion that meant, for a measure of time, she needn't think.

The boat moved slowly through the rigors of the small and tricky channel with an adroit and careful hand at the wheel. Another turn, as skillfully accomplished brought it nearer. Sleek, crisp lines of a master designer were apparent. The name at the bow became legible, and with it the familiar logo.

The craft was splendid, the logo startling, but it was the man at the helm that held her spellbound. She gaped, unnerved and wondering, long after he made the final turn toward her dock.

The skill that negotiated the narrow crooks in the river was as evident when the boat skimmed the side of the dock. Tilting back the billed cap that shielded him from the sun, the helmsman smiled at her. "Hello, Irish."

His voice was soft and deep and drawling, exactly as she remembered. The voice of her dreams.

A finger at the brim moved the hat another notch. "Permission to come ashore?"

"Rafe. Rafe Courtenay!"

The sloop rocked, a sail rippled. The logo of McCallum International shone in the late-afternoon light. Ducking under the swinging sail, he approached the coaming. "You were expecting someone else?"

A hasty shake of her head and a hairpin half-dislodged by her dervish twirling, spiraled to the dock. The mass of her hair tumbled about her shoulders in a wreath of burnished darkness. Brushing it impatiently from her face, she muttered as much to herself as Rafe, "I wasn't expecting anyone. One doesn't in this part of the bay."

"Ahh, then, since I'm not intruding, and not interrupting..." Taking a massive rope from its coil, he let it dangle from his fists. "Permission to come ashore?"

"Why are you here?" As she sidestepped his request, her hands were clasped before her to still their shaking. In her exile, she'd only just begun to deal with the rescue of Courtney McCallum, its consequences and its impact. She wasn't ready for his attitude and his questions. Nor for Rafe Courtenay, himself. "How did you find me? Why?"

"I'll answer all your questions." His smile changed from genial to patient. "But it would be easier over a drink, or a cup of coffee."

"I don't think so." Refusal spilled from her more emphatically than she intended. The training of a lifetime prompted an oblique and rambling apology. "What I mean is I don't think it's a good idea. I wouldn't be very pleasant company, or a proper hostess. It would be best for both of us if you turn about and go back to wherever you came from."

"You wouldn't be pleasant company? A proper hostess?" A shrug lifted his shoulders, straining the knit fabric of his shirt. "Fine, you needn't be either. This isn't a social engagement, I didn't come to be entertained."

"Then you're lost, this is a chance meeting, purely coincidental, and you'll be leaving right away." The acerbic drawl and her hurry to have done with him didn't keep her from noticing the sea had darkened his skin even more. That in his bronzed face, the flash of the smile that had been scarce in the desert was swift and brilliant, touching eyes as vivid as jade.

As she watched, the smile faded, his jeweled gaze regarded her. Softly, so softly she barely heard over the splash of the rippling tide, he asked, "What are you frightened of, O'Hara?"

Valentina bristled and reddened, and was grateful for her own excuse of blushing color from a day in the sun. "Frightened? I'm not. Why would I be? Why should I?"

"Do I frighten you?" An aberrant swell lifted the prow of the craft and set it rocking. He stood surefooted and as unmindful as if he stood on solid rock. "After you slept in my arms for most of two nights, are you suddenly afraid that I would harm you?"

Shaking her head and catching the sweep of her hair back all in a move, she stuttered a denial. "I never. I wouldn't."

"You dreamed, O'Hara." Rafe gripped the rope, wishing he could touch her and comfort her as before. "Disturbing dreams. And I held you until you slept at peace."

"Ahh, you're clairvoyant now." She wanted to back away, wanted to have done with this, but found herself rooted to the dock and imprisoned by the power of his gaze. Rejecting what he said, what he made her feel, she retaliated with scorn. "You claim to know the quality, if not the content of my dreams like some Gypsy fortune teller, and I'm to believe you? Don't be ridiculous."

"Truth is seldom ridiculous. And the truth is that in the desert your nights were pain and torment. Because it seemed to help, I held you until it passed."

"You lie." Once the nightmares had been frequent, but not in a long while. When they had begun again after her time with Rafe in the desert, she thought it was only here at the lodge. A backlash caused by the death of Edmund Brown. Resurgence of guilt she must face alone.

"You lie," she cried once more, desperate to disprove what she feared must be true.

Rafe looked steadily at her. As impervious to the insult as the roughening tide, but not her distress. His tone was low, his voice subdued. "You dreamed of David, O'Hara."

All the world receded. The dock did not rock beneath her feet. The breeze was still, the leaves quiet. No loons cried from the marsh in the darkening gray of the sun. "David."

His name was agony as fresh as the moment. A raw reminder that came too quickly on the heels of this day. She wasn't ready, her defenses weren't repaired. The key turned a second time in floodgates kept tightly closed. Except in her dreams. Except today.

Grotesquely familiar images resurfaced with the blinding power of a migraine. If the first had been a dagger to the heart, this was the battering ram she hadn't the strength to withstand. Hardly aware of her actions, she turned from Rafe quickly. But not before he'd seen that she'd paled. That her lips were stark and blue rimmed. That her eyes shone emptily above the purpling, ever more evident stains of lost sleep.

When she would have walked away, seeking escape from memory and from him, she found her way blocked. Rafe had leapt to the dock, permission to come ashore taken. His fingertips beneath her chin were callused but kind as they lifted her face. "Is that why you've come here? To grieve? To lock yourself away from the world while you sink into a quagmire of guilt for what can't be changed?"

"Don't!" Valentina closed both hands over his wrist, moving his fingers from her face. "You have no idea what you're saying. You don't understand. You can't."

"That's right, I don't know. At least not enough. And perhaps I don't understand, but I can." As he spoke she had looked away, her expression closed and brooding. A touch of their joined hands at her cheek returned her gaze to his. "I will before we're through."

"No." Her fingers curled, holding his hand against her flesh ever so briefly before she released him. "No," she repeated emphatically, even while she conceded his were the eyes that trespassed and confounded a waking nightmare. And his voice the gift of peaceful sleep.

Rebuffing the irrational need to step into his arms, to let Rafe Courtenay bear the brunt of her guilt and grief, she took a step back. Spine straight, shoulders square, her chin lifted by habit to a brave angle. "My problems are mine, and mine to confront alone."

"Alone. You use that word a great deal." At her look of askance, he continued grimly. "Is that why you look so worn? Because you let no one near you? Because there's no one to hold you through the night?"

"Stop! I don't want to hear this. I *won't* hear it." She took another step away, her stance regal. Only the ravages of the ordeal she'd chosen to suffer singularly betrayed her. "I'd like you to leave. If it satisfies your ego, pretend you came here by mistake. You were truly lost and wandered into my little part of the bay in one of the peculiar coincidences that prove life is stranger than fiction."

"Perhaps I have been lost," Rafe mused. "Perhaps I am. And if I am, how should I find my way back?"

He was teasing her, the subtle twist of his words did not escape her. She had no idea why he'd come. But for whatever reason, she was certain he wouldn't concede defeat so easily. An ache still coiled deeply within her, but she had regained her composure enough to play his game. "Finding your way back shouldn't be a problem. The simplest method would be to backtrack, taking the same route out that brought you in."

Rafe glanced at the sky. "It's getting dark, and landmarks never look the same from the opposite direction."

"Surely you have compasses and—"

"No." Rebuttal came quickly. "*The Summer Girl* was in the process of being stripped down for refurbishing and outfitting when I borrowed her for a while."

"Surely there are charts."

A smile that was almost angelic flickered over his face. A dismissive shrug accompanied it. "Forgot'em."

Valentina studied him, her glare narrowed and skeptical. "Are you sure you didn't run out of gas, too? Maybe you lost a sail, or the breeze."

"Maybe."

"We both know you aren't that big a fool, Rafe Courtenay," she snapped, her temper slipping away. "If you were, you'd be a hazard to everyone on the bay."

"I needn't be." A look over his shoulder directed her attention toward land. "If you have charts, that is."

"There are some," she admitted. "They're quite old." Relenting, only because she judged it the easiest way to rid herself of him, she sighed. "I suppose even an old chart is better than none in an emergency."

"I wouldn't refuse the offer of a cup of coffee while I check them. The tide's coming in, and the breeze has turned wet and frigid." As if on cue leaves rattled, sails snapped, the boat rocked and scraped against the dock. "See."

"I see."

"I missed lunch."

"You'll miss dinner, too. I don't cook."

"Except range fare."

"Right."

"A peanut butter sandwich would suffice."

"Don't push it, Courtenay."

"Wouldn't dream of it, Irish."

"Wise choice."

Her words were inhospitable. But as they strolled together from the dock, Rafe sensed a momentary subsiding of anguish.

Seven

Her home was not the typical cottage by the bay, and, even with a glimpse of its chimney tops, not what Rafe had envisioned. Though he couldn't say exactly what he'd expected, it wasn't this affair of stone and brick, with a roof of slate overhanging mullioned doors and windows. If the house was of country French design with connected carriage house and covered verandas, the grounds and gardens were purely English. A wonderful, disordered hodgepodge of sunny glen and graveled paths leading from shore. Then, in a perfect blend of cultures, in perfect complement, giving way to functional, simplistic formality nearest the house.

But not merely a house, Rafe realized as he veered through a hedge of clipped boxwood. A lodge, he deemed it as she led the way, her sneaker clad step making no sound on a winding avenue of brick-bordered stone. A hunting lodge from another era, another century, and authentic he would wager. And when he stepped onto an oval of lush, shorn grass circling the brick and stone ledge of a pool, he was hard-pressed not to stop and stare.

His astonishment was not for aged grandeur. Rafe was accustomed and comfortably familiar with both as a native Louisianan; and more and greater in the castles and keeps of Patrick's Scotland. It was not its haunting beauty, nor that such quiet majesty lay hidden in the wilds of the Chesapeake and the shores of Virginia, that intrigued him. It was that this, with all its grandeur and all its beauty, was the chosen refuge of Valentina O'Hara.

Another dimension. And, within its walls, perhaps, the key to the mystery that hovered like a cloak about her. Tearing his gaze from the structure, seeking some difference, an answer, Rafe looked to Valentina and found nothing.

Without pausing, immersed too deeply in her own response to the man and his physical presence to be conscious of his perception of her home, she took him quickly from garden to terrace to veranda. Massively cased doors swung on heavy hinges as she stepped inside a vaulted room.

"Make yourself comfortable." Avoiding his gaze, she gestured to a cluster of seats gathered before a fireplace laden with wood and lacking only a match. "I'll start the coffee."

"Don't bother."

"No bother," she called over her shoulder, as eager to put as little distance between them as to have something to occupy her time and her thoughts. "Or would you prefer tea?"

"Tea would be even better."

"Tea it is. I won't be a minute." Passing through an archway, she disappeared. Her voice floated back to him, a little strained, a little husky. "Then we'll see to the charts and set your course for home."

"Home," Rafe mused, and questioned which of a half dozen places he could truly call home. Did it matter? he wondered as he began to wander, unabashed, through this part of hers.

The great room, with its private alcoves and nooks, was plainly a work in progress. The main area and an adjoining loggia were an orderly study in polished wood, shining glass, and antiqued ceilings. Its half-hidden niches and crannies revealed a clutter of canvas sheets and ladders, carpentry tools, cans of paint and stain. Because it was Valentina's, an orderly clutter.

It was no surprise to him that the interior was only partially restored. Nor did it take great insight to know whose hands had patiently and painstakingly performed each chore. Even hidden away in this remote part of the estuary, she would not, could not fall into idleness. He had seen her in the desert, then a mountainside, and learned the demands she made of herself. He had watched her lie for hours, moving no more than to draw a breath or blink an eye. But for a purpose, with costly effort. For life, for death. For Courtney.

Grimly, he put the recollection aside. As she had, or had striven to do, with this and other times through her labors.

Restless, intrigued, he moved deeper into the room, reflecting on her thoroughness and yet another area of expertise. What he saw was more than busy work to quiet a troubled mind. Restoration of the venerable lodge was as much labor of love given by an intelligent and resolute woman, as panacea for the tribulations of conscience.

"Whatever works." Rafe heard the indifference in what would seem an uncaring verbal shrug, and recognized it for an oblique lie to himself. One without success. He wouldn't be here if the indifference were true. He wasn't quite sure why he cared, or how much. At this point, in a singular reversal for the icy-tempered Creole, he had no clear notion of his feelings for the woman he called O'Hara.

He'd begun by telling himself that he'd seen a need, one he felt obliged to answer in payment of a debt. But as he'd searched for her, exhausting every avenue, he admitted it went beyond obligation. When he came to Simon, challenging him, threatening a long-standing friendship, he knew obligation was the smallest part.

As he'd conceded to Simon, it was all too complicated.

In all his years, in all his relationships, he'd never felt this ambivalent about a woman. He either liked them, or he didn't. They were friends or casual lovers, or they weren't. Only one woman before had not fit the mold. But Valentina wasn't Jordana.

Valentina wasn't any woman. How did he deal with that? Must he, when he was only here to repay a debt?

"Is that all that brought you here, Courtenay?" His rasping question was a hollow knell, a false note even to his ears. Too much the realist to deceive himself, not ready to put a name to his unrest, he forced his attention back to the lodge and labors of remorse and love.

Remorse and love! Standing where she had stood, with the evidence surrounding him, he saw more clearly. This was the anguish he saw in her. What he heard in the nightmare she rode in sleep. It was here in the lodge, in the measure of her labor.

There would be years, yet, before the repair and refurbishing were complete. Years that would take her mind from the tragedies of her life.

But when the work is done? He turned in a broad sweep, his eyes closed. Yet even then he saw the exceptional workmanship, the precise attention to detail, the faithful preservation of its antiquity. His heavy lids lifted, his attention focused, seeing what his mind's eye had seen better. "When it's done?" his lips formed the question without sound. "What then, Valentina?"

Raking a hand across his face, he turned his thoughts to the conclusion he would wish for her. God willing, and by her own strength, in that time there would be some sort of closure. Some resolution for the guilt that drove her. And, God willing, by then she wouldn't be a part of Simon's grisly task force.

As much as peace, she needed gentleness in her life. But how did he make her see that when she lived by and with instruments of death?

But did she? Rafe turned again in a slow circle, only then becoming aware there were no gun cabinets, no gun racks in sight. No weapons of any sort. No records of death.

If there had been the expected trophies mounted on the walls, declaring a hunter's prowess, they had been removed and any vestige of their existence erased. In their stead were walls of shelves filled with books and wildlife carvings. Another rife with paintings and memorabilia of the sea. Turning, his gaze ranging from ceiling to floor, he imagined the room as it might have been, and discovered he liked better what it had become.

None of its masculinity had been lost. With leather and wood, it remained very much a man's room, yet one enriched by the comforting presence of a woman.

Was there comfort for Valentina among the memories she

brought here? Frowning, Rafe wondered if there could ever be.

The rustle of cloth, the tap of a step, the whisper of a drawn breath had him spinning, discovering that she watched him from the cathedral arch of the doorway. Her face was still, her eyes somber. With her head tilted, and one tattered shoe braced over the other, she looked more a watchful child than a wary woman.

At thirty-three and with her history, there was still an aura of innocence about her. As if the heartache that was an integral part of her was buried so deeply it never surfaced. He would almost have believed the theory, if he hadn't looked into her eyes and held her through the night.

"I was admiring your home."

"So I see. Thank you."

"I find it interesting, and quite...unexpected."

"I know. Not what one expects on the remote tributary. It belonged to one of my grandfathers. My father's grandfather, to be exact."

"A sportsman," Rafe ventured.

"Hunting, fishing." An eloquent lift of a shoulder drew taut a shirt grown as supple as silk with age. The hem, knotted at the waist, skimmed above the band of low riding jeans, revealing a ribbon of golden flesh and the narrow curve of her waist. "Collecting."

Intent on the little revelation, wondering how it would feel beneath the span of his hands, Rafe barely grasped the last thread of her comment. "Collecting?"

"Trophies, people, influence." Again the shrug, the caress of pliant broadcloth. The provocative glimpse. "And money."

Resisting the impulse to clear his throat, as his breath seemed to clot at its base, he lifted his gaze from the slender and elegant lines of her body to the immense and elegant vault of the towering ceiling. Even in its day, the lodge would have been neither simple nor economical to construct. "If what I've seen is any indication, the elder Mr. O'Hara collected quite a lot of the last, I would assume."

"Quite."

"Added to by each successive O'Hara." He returned his gaze carefully to her face. "With the exception of Keegan, who has made it his life's work to enjoy the spoils of his robber baron ancestry, while giving back an even greater portion to those who needed it.''

"How do you know that?" So few people were aware of her father's philanthropy, Valentina was startled that a virtual stranger should. Keegan O'Hara cultivated his image as spendthrift and rebel. It made the secrecy of his generosity possible and that much more rewarding. ''Not even my father's closest friends know. How could you?''

"Sources." The enigmatic answer was all Rafe intended to supply.

"The same sources, or should I say source, that sent you here?"

"Maybe."

Simon. There was a message on the answering machine in the kitchen. Only a name, given in response to a recital of the services of a business that did not exist. The code he sometimes used when there were matters to discuss that weren't critical, yet of concern.

Had he called to offer an excuse for a first and unheard-of infraction of his own immutable rule? Ruefully, in the face of what was apparently Simon's first default, she concluded Rafe Courtenay's determination must be as powerful as his body; his argument as eloquent as the emerald gaze that trespassed into her memory, her nightmares and her dreams.

Who else had ever bested Simon? How had Rafe? Why?

In the darkening of the day, as lights set by timers began to click on, a shiver of alarm skimmed over her. Yet was it truly alarm, she wondered with the unrelenting black-Irish honesty common to the O'Haras? Or was it premonition?

No! She wouldn't do this. Why borrow trouble when there was enough already? Pushing away from the arch, she moved further into the room.

"The red-throated loon." She spoke softly and curiously, unlike the woman who had challenged him not so long ago in a dusty camp in red rock country.

Rafe watched as she passed from dusky shadow into light. Rousing from his distraction as she approached, he heard himself muttering, ''What the hell?''

"The carving." Her nod indicated the miniature wood carving he didn't remember picking up. Had forgotten he held. "A red-throated loon."

"Of course, the carving." He stared blindly down at the fragile form, thinking only that distance and sunlight had been kind to her. Proximity and electric light leeched false color from her skin and laid bare the bruising toll of her life and work. Yet even then she was incredible. "Most incredible."

"He is handsome, isn't he? They're quite rare here. Occasionally a pair or a few will stop for a while on their winter migration to the Gulf. I heard one call from the salt marsh today. Look, this explains his name." Touching the small form, she traced the red half circle that described its striking feature. Her fingers brushed Rafe's, their warmth igniting a memory.

These hands had held her and soothed her and brought her comfort in the oblivion of her darkest hours. He'd told her this and she doubted him. But a part of her, the part that let him into her dreams, had always known. Her fingers curled over his with a will of their own as she found her gaze drawn to his face.

He was fire and ice as she looked up at him. The ice of control, the fire of something entirely different in his eyes. Tension returned; an awareness grew intense. Valentina was no stranger to desire. Once she'd known it, recognized it, shared it. Exulted in it. But for so long she'd kept herself aloof from the world, from people, from men, she was no longer sure. Appalled that she could make such wayward presumptions, when only a few weeks ago he had looked at her with distaste and contempt, she jerked her hand from him.

Unable to keep his gaze, she focused on the carving. A mistake, for all she could think was how capable were his fingers, how tender their touch.

"This is how he would look," she babbled and stared down at the loon. "In mating season...the loon, that is." She was only making it worse, yet couldn't stop. "We would never see him like this. The red-throated loon."

Somewhere behind her a scream began. Moving through the register of notes, it picked up steam.

"The teapot!" She wanted to run to the kitchen, but, with the greatest of effort, forced herself to walk.

Red-throated loon in hand, Rafe Courtenay stared after her, the fire in his eyes hotter still.

Certain she was only tired, determined she wouldn't act a fool, Valentina arranged a tea tray. Setting mugs, pots of cream and sugar, and a salver of lemon slices on it, she paused to consider, then made one last trip to the pantry.

Less than ten minutes later she found him standing before a window facing the bay, hands in pockets, his profile stark against the backdrop of panes. He was a handsome man. Hard and handsome, with hidden strengths and kindnesses. And, in that moment apart, it seemed right that he be there, in a room that suited him. A room she had created.

"The wind has turned, we're in for some weather."

He did not move or turn from the window, and even as he spoke Valentina heard the whispered moan of a gust among the eaves. "In that case, we'd best make quick work of our tea and get to the charts so you can be on your way."

"In that case, yes," he said simply, and strode to her, taking the tray from her. "The table by the window, or the fire?"

Attention riveted on Rafe, she hadn't realized the fire blazed briskly, its circle of heat inviting. The first of the season, and early, though the lodge was always cooled by its insulating walls of stone. If the wind was any sign, he had a frigid and wet journey ahead. He might as well be warm while he could. "The fire."

When they were seated across from each other, and he'd taken up a sandwich, he turned to her, intending a comment, the usual rejoinder common between them. Instead he found himself entranced, a teasing smile faltering before it formed. She stared into the fire, mesmerized by its dancing and ever-changing pattern. Her head was tilted, the spit-in-your-eye challenge gone from her. The red glow of the blaze was as kind as the sun had been, softening the pitiless edges of strain and melancholy, erasing the waxen cast lying beneath the blush of a day spent out-of-doors.

Here, now, in the gossamer illusion, in the flush of warming flames, she was as he'd never seen her. Lovelier than in the grace and mercy of remembrance, with eyes he once thought too dark to be blue, a thoughtful, impossible, improbable, wonderful sapphire. And lovelier still with her hair escaping its binding, tumbling around her face and shoulders in charming disarray. Blue-black and gleaming, its darkness catching the flickering light, a length of velvet spangled with stars. Though she sat unmoving, wisps and curls stirred by the beat of her heart, the depth of her breath, drifted against her cheeks and her neck, caressing her.

God help him, yes, she was lovely.

Beguiling. Enchanting.

Touchable.

As he would have her, always.

Illusion.

It was only that. A gift of the fire.

But, perhaps, someday.

Drawing himself again to reality and circumstance, he banished the seductive fantasy to the back of his thoughts. Yet he knew it would lie there in wait. An image he could never forget, never truly dismiss, branding his mind and his memory. Biding its time, whispering, gliding through his subconscious until it surfaced once more.

If he never saw her again, she would live on in him. A wayfarer, a stranger, who touched his life and left it changed. The measure of all women to come.

A stranger.

Shaking himself from this flight of fancy, reminding himself he was the cool, pragmatic Rafe Courtenay, with only his voice he drew her back to him from her own thoughtful sojourn. "You took me at my word." A nod and a gesture drew her attention and the thread of conversation to the safe, but not so mundane topic of food. "Almost, but not exactly."

Her face altered, not in a smile, but better, a glimmer of mischief. A slight tilt of her head accompanied a nod. Wisps and curls shimmered and shone and caressed. "Almost. But not exactly."

Verbatim repetition. Confession. Low and husky, amused. Enchanting him more.

"This from a woman who doesn't cook?" The concoction of thick slices of home-baked bread, roast beef oozing with a piquant, creamy sauce, and curling leaves of spinach nearly dwarfed his hand. "A meal fit for a king, with dessert for good measure! You don't expect me to believe any of this came from the local deli, do you?"

"Considering that there is none, hardly." More as a needed diversion than from hunger or thirst, Valentina sipped her tea and nibbled at a small cake.

"Is this something you learned in your childhood odyssey?" Part of what Simon had told him was more of her history. The unconventional education with the world as her classroom, its citizens of unique talents her teachers. "A skill acquired, I presume, as the skills I see in evidence here were acquired."

While his gesture encompassed the room, its scattering of tools and supplies, and the dish of small cakes, Valentina laughed. A charming note, and far too uncommon. "You can thank my mother's Irish influence for the sandwich and the cakes."

Valentina wondered what he would say if he knew the cakes he was admiring were an Irish favorite called petticoat tails, a corruption of *petite galette*—little cakes. "Credit her inborn belief that food needn't be complicated, but must always be good, for my simple and adequate culinary education. But both my mother and father are responsible for the rest of what you see here. And yes, it was part of our odyssey. We took a great deal for our own from every country, but in each case we tried to leave more."

"Building houses in depressed and rural areas of Appalachia, serving in soup kitchens in Chicago, tutoring and studying on reservations, initiating and funding a survival camp for problem children on a ranch in Montana. To name only a few." The sandwich was set down with only one bite taken from it. Hunger aside, this wasn't the time for food.

"Ahh," Valentina breathed a sigh. "Simon was thorough as usual, I see."

"Quite."

"Only for so far as he was able. He might tell you the facts. He might even catalog my parents' generosities, but none of us could begin to say, or explain, how much more was given to us. Freely and unstintingly."

"No 'even Steven'?"

"Some things are matchless."

"Yet you tried. No doubt, down to the last O'Hara."

Valentina set her cup on the table by the cake, which looked more as if a mouse had nibbled at it than a woman. "Of course." Her answer was short, but the frown that marred her forehead disappeared as she found in his look none of the cynicism she read into his words. "As you said, down to the last and littlest O'Hara."

"Quite a philosophy, giving back more than you take." Rafe put his own cup down, considered the sandwich, then reconsidered. "Keegan's or Mavis's or both?"

"Both." In a rapid change of mood, Valentina laughed again. The hearty trill only her family could draw from her. "But either will tell you it's more than a philosophy. It's the O'Haras immutable rule."

"That's twice." Rafe mused thoughtfully as his heart settled slowly back to its steady, pounding rhythm. "Twice in a space of five minutes. A veritable miracle."

"Twice?"

"You laughed. Something you do too seldom." If the sandwich hadn't been forgotten, it would be now. The sudden hunger that swept through him, then stayed to taunt and torment him, could never be sated by food. "I was right, you know, your mouth was made for smiling." His gaze lingered on her lips. Driven by irresistible impulse he leaned forward, brushing a crumb from them. His thumb tarried longer than was needed. "For smiling." His voice roughened, deepened. "And more."

Leaning back, putting distance between them, Valentina wrapped both shaking hands around her heavy mug. Lifting it to her lips, she found the heated rim cold after his touch. Desperate to turn the subject to safer ground, she observed wryly, "Thanks to dossiers and Simon, you seem to know a great deal about me, while I know nothing of you."

Mug in hand, taking his cue from her, Rafe leaned back, conceding the space she needed. "My life is an open book."

Valentina smiled, a small motion hidden by the bulk of the mug. A sip of tea calmed her as she moved it away. "Somehow I doubt that anything about you is as simple and obvious as an open book."

"For you it is. All you need do is ask. So," he settled deeper, more comfortably into the soft leather of the sofa, sipping the hearty brew. "What would you like to know, Valentina?"

"Oh, I don't know." A grimace meant for a cool smile made mockery of her indifference. "What you do. How you became so skilled in so many areas, in and beyond the business." *Who you are. Why you're here. What you want of me.* As the real questions of concern nagged at her, she watched him blandly, her true thoughts no more evident than his.

"My personal life is simple. I love a challenge, and a change of pace from the daily routine is more restful than idleness." Brief eye contact, a lifted brow, a nod, underscored a common bond. "Whatever skills I've acquired over the years are no more than a reflection of that. My job is as simple. I love the challenge, and I do whatever is needed by McCallum International."

"A simple job description often means a complicated responsibility, and, in this case, a more than competent man."

Rafe inclined his head, conceding one more point. "Another O'Hara philosophy?"

"An observation, Mr. CEO. My own."

"Based on…?"

"Public knowledge that under the dual guidance of Patrick McCallum and Rafe Courtenay, McCallum Investments of Scotland has grown into McCallum American and then McCallum International. That your name is as well known in certain circles as Patrick's. That half of the company would be yours, if you would accept it."

"You've done your homework."

"What I've said is common knowledge in business and trade journals," Valentina demurred.

"It has been in the past, but there's been nothing recently. So, you made the effort to search out information from back issues." Rafe sipped his tea and returned the mug to the tray. "Not an easy task."

"Not so difficult, either."

"Why? Why did you care?"

Valentina dismissed the depth and importance of her interest. "I was simply curious about the sort of man who would go to the limit, as you did, for the child of a friend."

"Courtney is more than the child of a friend. She's my goddaughter. A responsibility I take seriously."

"More than that, you love her, as you love her parents and her brothers."

"You learned all of this from journals?"

Valentina shook her head. "No journal could describe the lesson learned from the desert and the mountain."

"But you took it a step further."

"I suppose I did."

"Again, why?"

"I was curious." Scrubbing her palms over worn denim, she avoided meeting his look. "It shouldn't surprise you that I would be, given the circumstances."

Rafe wouldn't let her off so easily. "What circumstances are we discussing?" When there was no response after a moment he insisted gently, "Look at me, O'Hara. Look at me and tell me what circumstances."

Setting the tea aside, to forestall their betrayal of her agitation, Valentina laced her fingers and folded her hands about her knees. Drawing a long, slow, breath, she admitted only a partial truth. "I don't know."

"Did your research have anything to do with Courtney? Anything at all?"

Her folded hands clasped her knee closely, the bones hard against her palms. A lie would neither deceive nor deter him. "It had nothing to do with Courtney."

"Then why?" The same song, same verse, the same challenge, but too vital to abandon. "Why do you care?"

Rafe waited, seeing the tension in her, feeling it hum between them.

There it was, Valentina knew she should have expected it from the moment he stepped on shore. He hadn't become the person he was by skirting issues. Nor, she admitted, had she. Abandoning her blind study of her hands, she took up the gauntlet, giving back the same unrelenting challenge. "For the same reason you're here, I imagine. So, why don't you tell me."

As Rafe watched her, pensively, from the distance guarded

by the table, the wind moaned again in the eaves. A down draft sent a shower of sparks flying over the broad hearth. Light beyond the window darkened another subtle degree, before a barely perceptible smile flickered over his lips. "I would like to meet the man who taught you self-defense."

"You mean debate, don't you?"

"Debate, defense." Rafe gestured, a brief open-handed motion. "Often one and the same."

"I've had many teachers in the art of debate and defense. The best of both was Kim. An oriental without speech, who taught the daughters and sons of Keegan O'Hara to protect themselves, mentally as well as physically."

Rafe didn't question how one who couldn't speak could teach debate. He suspected there were other unique occurrences in her life, waiting to be discovered, awaiting an explanation. "Did Kim, who had no speech, teach you to turn the tables so adroitly?"

"He taught me to analyze, to find my best advantage, in all things."

"An intelligent, insightful man, whose teachings seem to have taken root."

"In all of us," Valentina agreed. "But of us all, only Tynan was the perfect student."

"The family philosopher."

"Among other things."

Rafe grinned and leaned an arm over the back of the sofa. A position that emphasized the breadth of his shoulders, the leanness of his body. "Given what I've heard and what I've learned, no one in his right mind would ever argue that an O'Hara—any O'Hara—was ever one dimensional."

"You feel you know us well enough to make that judgment?"

"All of you but one."

"Is that why you've come? To resolve your questions and render judgment?"

"*Judge* is your word, not mine." Rafe's reply was quick and easy, proving, as he had when they met, that he was as adept at verbal fencing as she.

An answer given too quickly, too easily. One Valentina

could not let pass. Rising, she walked to the window, standing in nearly the same place Rafe had stood.

The wind had died as suddenly as it had risen, bringing with it change. Wisps of smoky mist borne on warming air drifted through the channel from the bay. Touching, clinging, one layer building upon another, lying in a thick, impenetrable blanket over the estuary. The sun disappeared, the little that remained of the day was dark and murky. The lamp at her back shone in mullioned panes, mirroring the tilt of his head, the cast of his shoulders. He was a shape, a shadowy figure, no more. But she knew he watched her, as surely as if she could feel the sweep of his gaze.

The gathering mist crept from river to shore and billowed over the lawn. Window panes ran with rivulets of moisture before she turned to him with no trace of acrimony. Speaking fact, not accusation. "You judged me before."

"I was a fool, I won't be again."

"Is that why you've come here? To rectify a mistake?" Her arms were crossed beneath her breasts, as if by moving beyond the circle of the fire, she had grown cold. "I don't need your apologies, nor your regrets. I've been judged before, and more unfairly."

Rafe left the sofa, crossing swiftly to her. Taking her by the shoulders, he drew her nearer. With only the heat of their bodies touching, mingling, tension sang again in a higher octave. "I didn't come to rectify an error. I didn't come to apologize. And I didn't come out of regret. I came because I had to."

"That makes no sense." His hands were heavy on her shoulders. A hunger she hadn't felt in a long, long while stirred in her. Shaking free, in quiet panic, she backed away. From new-old feelings. From the man who haunted her nights and her days. Dreaming or awake. "I don't understand."

His hands hovered in the air after she'd left them. For the space of a heartbeat he was tempted to reach out again, to draw her back to him. But if he did, if she came willingly to his embrace, there would be no denying desire. No going back.

It was too soon. There was too much to be resolved. Too much to understand. Curling his fingers into his palms, he let his fisted hands fall to his sides. He wouldn't touch her again. Not until she came to him unfettered by the past.

Fog tapped at the windows. Sound perceived not heard. Coming on the little cat feet of Sandberg's poetic eloquence, it sat on silent haunches. When the sleeping wind woke, it would move on. But not yet. For now it was his ally, sealing them away from the world. "I think you do, Valentina," he murmured softly. "I think you understand better than you wish. I think you know what you want. What we both want."

She backed away another step. "You have no idea what I... No! You're wrong. No! No! No!"

Rafe advanced a step and was pleased when she stood her ground. "Yes." Breaking his brand new rule, and because there was no help for it, he traced the line of her cheek from temple to the corner of her mouth. "When I make love to you, it will be because we both want it."

Catching his wrist in a firm grasp, she stared up at him. "I'm not into one-night stands."

"Nor am I. What's between us could never be resolved in a night."

"You sound so certain." She felt his fingertips leave her face as he took his wrist from her circling clasp. But the memory of his touch, the throb of his pulse, lingered on.

"I've been certain from the moment I held you and comforted you, wishing I could dream your dreams for you."

"You would dream my dreams?"

"If I could."

"Even when they're of another man?"

"Especially then."

Bewildered, deeply touched, she spun away from the intensity of his gaze. A new understanding began to evolve in her mind. "There are compasses aboard *The Summer Girl*, aren't there?"

"There are compasses."

"And sextants?"

"And sextants."

"Charts?"

"More than I would ever need."

Valentina crossed her arms again, her fingers clutching at her sides. "You never intended to leave."

"Not so soon. Not without you."

She had no idea what he meant, but she dared not ask. In any case, he couldn't go now. In this fog it would be suicide, even for the most experienced seafarer. "You seem to have this all worked out. Did you order the weather, as well?"

Rafe chuckled, diffusing the tension only a portion. "That I left to God and Mother Nature."

"How kind of you." She spun to face him again, mockery dripping from her drawling words.

"How kind of them to spare me another battle," he countered.

"I've only one renovated bedroom. *Mine.*"

"And how kind of you to offer to share—"

"You're out of your mind, Rafe Courtney."

"—but the sofa will suffice." Closing the little distance between them, he bent to kiss her, quickly, gently. Daring only a taste of her. While her mouth still trembled, he stroked her hair, murmured something too softly to be comprehended and returned to the table and the repast she'd made him.

The tepid tea had been drunk, his sandwich gathered up and devoured, before Valentina gathered her scattered wits.

Eight

The beach was a narrow, primordial strip of sandy soil separating earth from this briny passage to the sea. One small part of thousands of miles of curling, meandering merges of land and water marking the beginning and the end of the Chesapeake.

At the edge of a salt marsh, a great blue heron splashed and fluttered as it speared a breakfast catch. Without turning or slowing his pace, Rafe identified the sound. One that had grown commonplace in the time he'd spent walking the shores of Valentina's retreat. He wondered, apropos of nothing but a ranging, questioning mind, if there was a season of the year, or a country in the world in which this skinny-legged Ichabod did not stand watch over dawn.

He wondered, as well, if it were an unwritten dictum of man and life that a stroll on the beach, any beach, should offer succor for body and spirit. And as he wondered he understood, as he had each of the three mornings he'd walked this walk, why Valentina came back to it time and again after each call from Simon. Returning to recover, to recoup. If never truly healed.

On this, the day he meant to be the last on her small island, he found her where he knew he would always find her in this hour encompassing dawn and day. The curving easternmost point, the end of her mile long expanse of shore, drew her as inevitably, as surely, as if it were her lodestar. While the river churned and swirled on its way to empty into the broad expanse of the Greater Chesapeake, she stood at its edge, her slender figure delineated in perfect detail by dancing reflection, her face raised to the sun just lifting from the rimline of the horizon.

Loath to disturb her reverie and the thoughts that took her so far from him, he approached slowly, his footsteps soundless. Choosing his customary seat, he settled on a half-petrified log of driftwood washed on shore only God knew when, or from where. As light burst fully upon them, bright and white with hues of sunrise giving way to a clear cerulean sky, he waited.

Affronted by the intrusion, a red-jointed fiddler crab scuttled away. Its trail a telltale line of crumbling, shifting sand dotted with bits of white quartzite and black and cream-colored chert. From a neighboring mix of trees, in a great flapping of wings, a bald eagle lifted from an aerie sprawled among the towering, uppermost limbs of a dying conifer. A magnificent treasure, a beautiful spectacle, strafing silver-crested ripples.

While the eagle soared, tiny beach creatures and sand dwellers tied to the earth scurried and hurried in their fashion. Fish leapt, sparkling rainbows in the light. Shells washed from deeper water tumbled on shore. There were bird calls and birdsong raised in morning symphony. But none were the red-throated loon, rarest of the rare on the bay. Valentina's favorite.

As he waited and watched, the lap of the tide and the distant sea kept the rhythm of the day. A muted whisper, like the hum captured by a shell clutched to the ear of a child.

Time passed slowly, yet seemed not long. Warm air, borne in the night on wind and fog of the first evening, wafted in stalled currents around him. And with every increment of the climb of the sun, grew warmer still. One more day of temporary reprieve from the promise of premature autumn. A reprieve mildly refuted by the clarion cries of a chevron of tundra swans winging across the horizon in early arrival from the Arctic.

"Once the estuary was as clear as the sky, and even the rarest bird was plentiful."

Drawn from his pensive drifting, Rafe abandoned his idle watch of morning by the bay. Valentina had deserted the point of her meditation to cross the sand to stand by him.

"In the days when the lodge was built the bay was different," she explained. "I'm told one could stand chest high in water and see the shells and sea creatures and recognize which fishes were nibbling at toes or heels."

"Until the world and modern ways discovered its riches." Responding, looking, listening, Rafe made his own discovery. One he made anew each day. She was lovely in the morning light, with her hair still tossed by sleep and her mouth easy of stress. Barely restraining himself, barely keeping his mouth from exploring the dewy softness of hers, as he hungered for more than the taste of his single kiss, he clung to the thread of conversation. "Progress. If pillage of land and sea can be counted progress."

Intent on Rafe, Valentina only shrugged, abandoning an old thorn in the modern conscience for a more immediate interest. "You slept well?" An expression surprisingly like a smile played at the corners of her mouth. "Three nights on the sofa and you haven't taken to hobbling hunchbacked or scuttling sideways like a crab."

For three days he'd been her uninvited guest. Because he'd stayed too long helping her with renovations to the ceiling, because they'd sailed too long on *The Summer Girl*, or fished too long in the marshy ponds. Because the tide had turned, leaving the river too shallow for the sloop to traverse, or night had fallen, making passage too uncertain. Because this task or that, once begun had not been completed.

Each reason, each pretext, however flimsy or flawed, had been accepted with more grace than it merited.

For three nights he'd lain on the sofa a stone's throw from her room, listening for dreams that never came. For three days he'd risen with her, given her these few minutes of solitude, then walked with her and talked with her. As she went about her days, he'd worked and played by her side, as if it were natural that he be there. As if he would never leave.

"I slept well." He spoke neither lie nor truth, but an evaluation of three hours or, sometimes, four. Enough.

Returning her smile, he found the brightness of the pristine morning turned her tumbled hair to a gleaming cloud. And resolutely he tamped back the familiar longing to bury his hands in it and feel its silken glide through his palms. Instead of addressing one need, he answered another by linking his fingers through hers to draw her down to sit by him.

Her shoulder touched his. The length of a thigh, left half-naked beyond the frayed fringe of her cutoffs, brushed the corded seam of khakis he'd retrieved from an ever-prepared duffel kept on board the boat. As his own body tensed in response, the rise of her breasts seemed to stop in a broken breath. Her fingers trembled against his. Just for the moment, she seemed suspended. Mesmerized, beguiled. Yet when he looked at her, his probing gaze drawn inevitably to hers, her eyes were clear and calm.

And he knew he had only imagined. Perhaps wished. "And you?" he asked in a tone that was solicitous, revealing little of his disquiet. "Have you slept well?"

"Quite well." Turning her face away, she regarded her bare toes with great interest.

In another circumstance, with another woman, Rafe would have thought this the advance and retreat of a coquette's seductive ploy. But not here. Not with Valentina. In all his life, he'd never met a woman like her. Never so complex nor so innocent. Never so many intriguing qualities, so many talents. So many psyches in one.

Which was she today and every day as she walked the shore? Perhaps a barefoot and distracted beachcomber who never collected a shell? No, he decided quickly, certainly. More simply, a beach walker, seeking solace, collecting melancholy thoughts instead.

"What do you think of when you come here, Valentina?" He wondered aloud, gathering her hand closer into his grasp when she would have pulled away. "What are you thinking now?" In a voice so low it was nearly lost in the sounds of the morning, he asked, "What makes you so solemn and quiet?"

"This and that." A toss of her head, meant to belittle the significance of her thoughts, was unconvincing. "Sense and nonsense. Nothing earthshaking."

"Do you think of David?"

Valentina recoiled, a slight move, a token distancing. She'd known from the first that questions of David were inevitable. Yet she hadn't expected it here, or now. Nor that his interest would be as unstructured, so unspecific. Specific would be easier. The who, the what, the when, where and why of it. Direct questions, allowing decisive answers, with little need to expound, and less to hurt.

"I think of him." Her feet shifted, scuffing deeper into sand. "Of course I do. I always will."

For all her reserve, something in her tone caught at Rafe, a desperate resolve that nagged at him. He hadn't intended to probe, or delve into more than she would volunteer, but now he knew he must. "Tell me what you were thinking just now. Was it of David? Only David?"

"Yes! Always." Catching her lower lip between her teeth, she shivered at her own half truth. The innate O'Hara honesty had her adding and qualifying when she never intended it. "But lately, mostly...today..."

"Today...?" he prompted, encouraging the faltering revelation.

Now that she'd begun, there was no turning back. "I was thinking of dreams I haven't dreamed." *And eyes that weren't David's. A consoling voice not David's. A comforting touch not David's.*

"As you did in the desert?"

Valentina gave no answer. Not even the O'Hara honor could compel her to speak the inexplicable.

"But you have dreamed here, as well?" In the desert, or a stone lodge by the bay, Rafe would name them nightmares, the subconscious agony of a soul. Never dreams.

"This time."

"This time," he mused, letting the full import of the terse comment sink in. "This time, but not before?"

She was silent for so long he'd begun to think she wouldn't

respond. When she did there was evasion, a hesitant quality in her manner, as if they'd trod on forbidden ground. "Not in a long, long while."

"Then you've come full circle."

"In a way."

Her terse acknowledgment told him nothing. A subconscious stepping back into the past to deal with something left unresolved would be healing. Sinking into the bog of yesterday to avoid tomorrow would be worse than disastrous. For Valentina. For him.

"The dreams came in the desert." Hazarding a guess, he added, "As they have in other places, before other assignments."

"Some. Yes." She would offer no more than minimal candor.

"And then here for the first time, as you said, in a long, long while."

"Circumstance." Falling silent, she left him to make what he would of the single word.

They were still again, and quiet. Sand, stirred by a lazy dust devil darting over the shore like a ground-hugging land shark, sifted sand over their feet and ankles. The fiddler peeped from a burrow. Lulled into courage by their silence, he whisked to another. A heron stalked the waterline, scaly legs like toothpicks, moving, bending, graceful in fastidious slow motion.

The great bird had moved from sight, and Valentina had been given a moment of respite before Rafe ventured the most telling question. "You dreamed here again, and then they stopped. Will you tell me when?"

She had been staring out over the water, now she turned to face him. The clear calm in her eyes had become dark and thoughtful. "I don't have to tell you. You know."

"Then you haven't lain awake fighting sleep to ward them off while I've been here?"

"I did, the first night."

"But in the end you slept?"

"In the end."

"The horror that troubles your sleep never came?"

"Never."

"Why?"

Why? With a sudden shiver, Valentina looked away. That was the crux of it. The crux of everything. *Why*, of all possible choices, had she chosen law enforcement as her life's work? *Why*, on that dark and fateful day, hadn't she been taken hostage instead of David? *Why* hadn't she done what was needed to save him? *Why* did dreams of that day begin again at the lodge after so long?

Why, indeed, had they disappeared when Rafe Courtenay came to her?

She strove for rigid composure, but knew he heard the long, ragged breath that shuddered through her. She knew he sensed the strain in her. Moving restlessly, with her toes she traced and erased and retraced random patterns in the sand. "Who can say or explain? I can't begin to define or interpret the rationale of any of this." Pausing, she lost herself for a little time, exploring, weighing truth and reality.

Then, rousing, turning from within, she looked at him long and thoughtfully. "I suppose—" she stopped short, a small frown only a quirk of her brow. "I think... No!" she corrected adamantly, yet softly, this time with total candor. "I don't think, I believe. I believe simply knowing there's someone who understands, someone who cares, who would take my dreams from me and face the anguish of them in my stead, if only he could, has eased their hold."

He heard caution in the stilted, carefully worded confession. She wouldn't be so foolish as to say this fugue of the night had been vanquished forever. Nor would he. But were it not an end, they would deal with what they must. Together.

Covering their joined hands with his, he began. "A moment ago you sounded almost angry. Are you sorry the dreams are gone?"

Averting her head vehemently, using the curtain of her hair as her shield, she said, "I'm not sorry. I don't want to keep reliving it again and again. But I don't want to forget. I can't. I mustn't."

"Is that why you won't forgive yourself, Valentina?"

With startling intuition he'd laid bare her fear that in time, in the life-or-death essence of her work, if she let herself grow jaded, David would become simply a failure. The first, perhaps one of many. "I don't know," she admitted. "Maybe."

"Forgiving doesn't mean forgetting, Valentina. Nor does it diminish the loss. Neither does having done with the punishment and going on with your own life."

"Is that what you think I'm doing? Punishing myself?" She still would not look at him. Couldn't look at him. "In your infinite Creole wisdom, have you determined that I'm purposely perpetuating the guilt of David's death by not going on with my life?"

Rafe turned her palm in his. A broad, masculine thumb stroked the scars and calluses left by the care and drudgery spent on the restoration of a dwelling. Endeavors better spent on the restoration of her spirit. Ignoring the bristle of contempt, he refused to back away. "Isn't that exactly what you do here?"

Valentina snatched her hand from his. Bounding from the log, she stalked to the water's edge. The bristle of contempt became the flash point of defense. Her arms were close about her, convulsing fingers driving into the flesh of her shoulders. "You don't know anything about it. Not who David was, or what he meant to me, or how and why he died."

"That's true. I don't know who he was or how he died. But I would be a fool not to realize that you loved him. That you were *in* love with him. I hope…"

"My, my, what an intelligent man you are, Rafe Courtenay." Weary anger threaded through the interrupting mockery. "McCallum International is truly fortunate to have such an insightful man at its helm."

"I hope," Rafe resumed patiently, "the day will come when you tell me the rest. On that day, perhaps, you can forgive yourself and begin to live again."

"I don't have to tell you," she said, lashing out. "You've read my dossier enough to have memorized it. You know what I did before Simon recruited me. You know where. All you need do to discover the rest is go there. Go to the city's papers or libraries. Check their morgues, read the back copies you find in them. The years shouldn't be hard to figure. You'll find the story there, every gory detail, in black and white."

"I could have, and I can," Rafe agreed mildly. "But I won't."

"Why not? Why not spare me the inquisition and answer your morbid curiosity in one effort?"

"No papers from any morgue will tell me what I really need to know...the one really important factor."

"And what would that be?"

"You, Valentina. The details of this as it relates to you. Only and always you."

"Me! After your less-than-auspicious beginning with the cold-blooded, coldhearted bitch who can take the shot no one else would dare? Who walks away without a care or a backward glance? A freak." This time her mockery was tenuous, and for its bitterness, not quite so biting.

"Amazing, isn't it?"

"What does it mean?"

"Whatever we decide to make of it." Easing back a mental pace, determined not to press a point before she was ready, Rafe forced a smile. He'd heard the camp scuttlebutt, felt the reluctant and resentful awe of men who regarded her exactly as she described. Cold-blooded, coldhearted. An aberration, if not a freak. A necessary evil. A view he'd shared. But as with Ranger Joe Collins, Commander Richard Trent, and a majority of the others—a view that had changed.

"That's it?" Confounded and unsettled, she snapped, "You harass me in the desert, rejecting my plans, interrupting my usual procedures. When I leave, you follow me more than halfway across a continent. Next you browbeat secret and privileged information from a man as closemouthed as God. Then you invade my harbor, set up camp in my home, disrupt my life, play havoc with my mind and my thoughts, and that's all you have to say?"

"For now." He answered the tirade mildly, when all he could think was how magnificent she was. How brave.

"You are the most maddening man I've ever met." A finger pointing emphatically drove home her point. "No one has made me so angry in years. Not since—" paling, she faltered "—not since..."

Unable to complete the unexpected thought, unwilling to face the man who provoked it, she stalked away. In her confusion she found herself at the point again. The last place she wanted to be, but the way home would take her past Rafe. All she could do was hope he would choose to leave the shore soon, and in the meantime, she must wait him out.

She knew her hopes and her plans weren't to be as his hands came down on her shoulders. When she would have objected and flinched away from his touch, he stopped her with a gentle command.

"Stay." Keeping her, even as he asked, he drew her back against him. With his lips brushing over her temple, he murmured, "Please."

"Rafe…"

"Don't." The touch of her body, the wildflower scent, the heat of his own need intoxicated. "Don't push me away. I didn't come to make you angry, and I promise not to hurt you."

She was unyielding in his arms, her body taut, resisting the tempting strength of his. In the measure of days, she knew little about him. Yet in the measure of men, she was certain he would never hurt her. Would never *intend* to hurt her. As she never intended to hurt.

"This won't work," she protested, with no definite thought to what she was saying or what she meant.

"It will." He held her tighter, with cherishing care that was comforting and undemanding. "I know this is difficult, that painful circumstances must be faced and resolved. But give it a chance. Give me a chance. Let me help you deal with what you must. Let me go with you into whatever hell you consigned yourself to for causing David's death."

The ragged gasp she caught was long and rasping, but she didn't pull away. She was too unnerved to move. Too devastated. Then slowly her head turned, left, then right. Then left again. Not in denial, but in pain. "You said you didn't know. You said…"

His arms crossed over her breasts, the back of one hand stroked the smooth plane of her cheek. His voice was warm assurance in her ear. "I don't know. I said I wouldn't and hadn't delved into your past."

"David wasn't in the dossier, and Simon might break his silence and his own rules by telling you where to find me, but he wouldn't tell you about David."

"Simon didn't tell me."

"Then who?" She turned in his embrace, to stare darkly up at him.

"You, sweetheart."

"Only his name!" But how could she know there had been no more? How could she guard against the guilt that emerged in the night? What private memories had she babbled? What secrets?

Reading concerns so clearly shown on her face, Rafe wanted only to ease her distress. "Some things are spoken more clearly with actions than words." Lifting a hand from her waist where it had fallen when she turned, he stroked the cords of tension at her throat. "The dream was the beginning. These tell the rest."

Taking her hand in both of his, he opened her curled fingers exposing worn and callused palm. "And these."

"We've discussed my work habits before."

"Yes." Nodding, he released her, but didn't move away. "We have."

Looking down at the sand, she muttered, "You read too much into a little."

"Do I?"

When she didn't answer, a finger at her chin lifted her face to his again. "You're an honest woman, Valentina O'Hara. Except for Jordana McCallum, and except in matters regarding yourself, the most honest woman I've ever known."

She didn't want to like the soothing touch of his fingers at her throat. She didn't want to see the blaze of need in his eyes. She didn't want to go where this was leading. But nothing in the world could have stopped her from asking hoarsely, "So?"

"So, once again, my honest O'Hara," Rafe teased softly, taking her gently where they both knew they must go. He was so close he could see the shallow rise and fall of her breasts beneath the taut gathers of the cotton T-shirt bunched and tied upon itself at the waist of denim cutoffs. He watched the sweep of her lashes and measured the visible throb in the tender hollow at the base of her throat. "Do I read too much into a little? Honestly?"

Suddenly this was not about David, or the past. This was Valentina and Rafe. Here and now.

Her lips shaped her answer without sound. With a shake of her head, and another sweep of her lashes, she met his intense study levelly. Walls built and rebuilt again came tumbling down for the last time. "No." This time her voice was stronger. Then surer. "It isn't too much."

Then she was in his arms. As their lips met, neither would ever remember who had reached for whom. Nor care whose body flowed first against the other. With hungering mouths plundering and wondering hands caressing, the world could have faltered without notice.

The contact of their bodies was as powerful as an inferno. Its heat an arc of molten desire that burned and seared. A passion that, once unleashed, would know no ebb. No matter where. No matter that there were other issues to be resolved. Issues and concerns.

Because he was a man of principle and of honor, Rafe was first to move, first to force himself to back away. He was pale beneath the darkness of his skin. The battle to resist the driving desire drew the mouth that had kissed her so completely, so fiercely, to a thin, grim line. There was hunger in his eyes, yet he looked at her, gravely. "You were right."

"I was? I am?" Struck by the certainty that he was going to agree this nameless passion between them was a mistake, she stumbled in retreat. Water lapped at her ankles and swirled unheeded about her toes. Giddy delight turned to pulsing pain. Her lips, still warmed by his kiss, were ridged in desperate restraint. Gathering the shreds of her pride, she met his piercing gaze with a lackluster calm. "How so?"

"I've been an arrogant fool." The declaration was blunt and grating.

"Perhaps we both have been." When she would have retreated deeper into the water, bleakly anxious to put distance between them, his fingers lashing out to circle her wrist wouldn't allow it.

"I was arrogant. I was the fool, never you, Valentina. I judged you when I knew nothing of you. Measured you against standards never meant for one of your experience. I went to the desert and to the mountain prepared to use you, any way I could. Even as I abhorred what you were." Correcting himself he said, "What I wanted to believe you were."

Valentina remembered the hard, cold man who had accepted her skills and expertise, but made it no secret that he didn't trust her choices. The same man who had ridden the desert with her, scaled a mountain of stone. Meeting challenge with challenge, coming, at last, to lie by her side for hours without question. Until the fateful shot was fired. "You distrusted me. I was everything you disliked, and then?"

With a wandering hand he brushed the hair from her shoulders, his fingers lingering at the tender flesh at her nape. "First I listened with more than my prejudices." When she didn't cringe from him, when he saw in her dark and lovely gaze no lingering malice for past sins, he murmured, "And then I held you in my arms and learned the truth."

Fighting back a shiver and the need to turn her lips into his palm, she responded, "Only part of the truth."

"Enough." His fingers were a delicate vise about her neck, drawing her to him. "Enough about myself. Enough that I had to find you." The weight on his heart lifted as she glided gracefully into his arms. "Enough," he whispered, "for this."

Valentina knew she shouldn't go so willingly into his embrace. Much had been left unsaid, much unresolved. Yet there was a desperateness in her, a deep-rooted sadness that reached for the lost beauty of love. Reached greedily, though Rafe had not uttered the word.

As she had not.

As they never would.

But they could pretend. For a while she could make believe that she was whole, that she was worthy.

For a while, with his lips on hers and his body enticing, with clamshells and mussel shells and shells with names like broken angel and fallen angel tumbling at their feet...they could pretend.

She made no protest when he swung her into his arms. No protest when he carried her from the water, over dune and dock, through garden and lawn. None when he stepped through the door of her bedroom for the first time.

Kissing her with renewed passion that maddened and frightened and excited, he set her on her feet. Only to draw her back again into an embrace so close, so tight it seemed to promise forever.

"We'll go to whatever hell it takes. Together, Valentina."
His pledge was a rasping groan. "But, before hell there is
heaven."

As if it were no effort and his hands were magic, her shirt
was untied and drifting to her feet. As easily, as surely, as
magically, the rest of her clothing and his were scattered
across the floor.

Taking her by the hand he strode the length of the room to
her bed. At its edge he stopped drawing her closer. His eyes
were green fire as he looked down at her, seeking, discovering,
his marauding gaze a caress. His kiss soothed the blush of her
cheeks, his fingers stroked the mounting ache in her breasts.
When he bent to kiss away the yearning havoc he'd made,
with tender suckling he created more.

Valentina swayed and gasped and heard a cry. Not of pain,
but rapture, and knew it was her lips that formed it as her
body responded. And suddenly what was more than she had
ever known was not enough.

Grasping his head, her fingers combing through his hair,
dragging his lips from her breasts to her mouth, she kissed
him. Her body curled into his, her nakedness inflamed and
inflaming in the tiny frisson of time before she moved away.
Taking his hand, she drew him down with her, down to her
solitary bed.

Cotton sheets were like silk at her back, Rafe's touch teasing madness on her body. He was a man who understood a
woman's needs. He knew and discovered the responsive
curves, the secret and vulnerable clefts. Each drifting exploration, each tender caress left her writhing and throbbing, tumbling deeper into the whirlwind of lust and love.

When she could bear no more, catching his wrist between
trembling fingers, she drew his hands to her lips. Brushing a
kiss over his knuckles, her tongue tasting the salt of his flesh
drew a groan from him.

Her smoldering gaze collided with his. There was the grim-
ness of determined restraint in him. What more would come
of this would be her decision. Tracing the tips of his clever
fingers with her kisses, she made her choice. "Make love to
me. Make love to me, now."

When he hesitated, and it seemed he would move away, she held him tighter, keeping him. "Please."

And still he waited as his gaze left hers, to glide over her making love with each fleeting glance. His chest rose and fell in a long, stuttering sigh. His look was a strange mix of possession and bitterness, his voice hollow and deep. "I'm not David, O'Hara."

Sunlight fell through squares of arched windows, casting patterns of light and shadow over her bed. Etched half in shade, half in light, his face was a study of bright strength and dark beauty. Two halves of the same face. Two qualities of the same man.

Rafe.

Releasing him, she raised a questing hand to his cheek. Like a sightless child, with a butterfly touch her fingertips skimmed over the slight hollow of his temple, his brow. Brushed over a fringe of lashes and down the bridge of his nose. She lingered a bit at the soft parting of his lips, and smiled at his roughly drawn breath.

Her palm curled at his chin, then slid over his jaw and into his hair. With a fistful as her leverage, she drew him closer. And when he did not resist, closer still. "I know," she whispered as her lips almost touched his. "Dear heaven, I know."

With her body inviting and arching to receive him, a single word seduced him.

"Rafe."

Two more sealed his fate.

"My love."

"I know a place."

"Do you?" Valentina nestled back against him, her arms crossed over his at her waist. The sun had lifted above the window, and, as they stood watching, the day descended into afternoon.

"Umm-hmm." With his cheek Rafe brushed a dewy dampness from her shoulder and kissed the curve of her throat. "Sandy beaches stretching for miles. Glittering like diamonds by day, rivaling the stars at night. And surf, foamy and white, capping waves as blue as your eyes. A place where the wind sings in palms and palmettos, and each day is as warm and soft as a kiss."

"Sounds like heaven."

Rafe chuckled, and kissed her again. "Close. But no cigar."

Settling for what she had, without turning, Valentina caught at the lobe of his ear tugging him to her waiting mouth. When she could think again and speak again, she asked dreamily, "How close?"

"Eden."

"Eden?" she repeated. "Truly?"

"Truly."

For a long while they were quiet again, each thinking, remembering. Each watching the passage of the day between kisses.

The habitual and inevitable blue heron, standing on one foot at the edge of the lawn, shivered then fluffed and preened. Strolling in imperious majesty across the yard, he stopped before their window. Cocking his head this way and that, he peered toward the bedroom panes. Then, seeing only a handsome bird like himself, he glided on.

Smiling at the great bird's antics, Valentina asked, "Are there blue herons?"

"On Eden? Hundreds."

"Good. There should always be herons."

Rafe didn't move, didn't blink, didn't breath. "Will you go there with me?"

"Yes." No questions. No quibbling. Simply, yes.

A smothered sigh whispered from him. "The tide is in. *The Summer Girl* should sail soon."

"She should, but..."

The caveat drifted to nothing as he turned her to him. Looping his thumbs beneath the lapels of the gossamer robe she wore, he slipped it from her. Swinging her naked body into his arms, he kissed her again as if he could never kiss her long enough, or hard enough.

Taking her to her bed, lying with her there, he finished for her, "But we have time."

Nine

Sails billowed, catching a benevolent breeze as *The Summer Girl* glided over a calm sea. Shore was only a craggy line against the horizon. The day was bright and warm, the afternoon sky cloudless.

This small drift of time was all Rafe would have wanted of it. Quiet, uneventful. The captain and his one man crew at peace.

Chuckling softly to himself at his own misnomer, Rafe regarded his "one-man crew." Valentina lay as she had for more than an hour, with her face turned aside, marking their passage by the changing vista, lapsing in and out of restful languor.

A rest well earned that pleased him immensely.

One day at sea had proven she was a worthy and knowledgeable seaman. Two days and she had become invaluable. In three, as the sea seduced, she had fallen into a natural, rhythmic routine. Her hands were willing and strong, her smile quick. Sun and wind and reflection had turned her face and body a light flush of bronze. And, hardworking, spirited crewman or not, as she whiled away a lazy afternoon in a swimsuit that had seen better days, no man in his right mind would call her anything but a woman.

Filling sails creaked and snapped, the sloop rocked for a furious moment as a rogue wave rushed quickly by. As *The Summer Girl* settled into a calm glide, roused from her drowsy drifting, Valentina shifted and turned and found him watching from his station at the helm. "Hi."

Rafe grinned at the lazy greeting, his gaze never leaving her. "Hi, yourself, sleepyhead."

Swinging her feet to the floor and brushing the wild disorder of her hair from her face, she smothered a yawn. "Did I sleep for long?"

"Only a short while."

"Short this time, but I don't think I've slept so much or so well in my life." An unruffled sigh and a careless shrug almost dislodged the wisp of cloth that covered her breasts, but she hardly noticed. "It must be the sea."

"Must be."

"I can't remember the last time I sailed."

Rafe said nothing, letting her take the conversation where she would.

She watched a half dozen small ripples of a calm sea rush by, imagining their frothy caps of white as they rose up to wash a distant shore. "We always returned to the sea. After each family odyssey and each adventure, the bay was there, waiting for us." Smiling, she mused fondly, "My dad insists there's pirate blood as much as the robber baron blood running in our veins."

This account of the robber barons had been described in her dossier. With it, the family history, the untapped influential connections, the wealth. But no sheaf of papers could express the affection he heard, the closeness of family ties.

Yet when she grieved, she grieved alone.

"No matter where we've been, or what we've done, we always come back to it. As kids it was to sail and scavenge the shore. As adults..." In a preoccupied gesture, she stroked a fingertip down the line of her throat. "I suppose it's simply in answer to a need in us."

"To celebrate." He risked an observation. "Sometimes to heal."

"Heal?" A sudden frown washed over her face, then was gone as suddenly. "Yes." She nodded. "Sometimes."

Rafe said nothing more.

"Only two of us have broken the habit. Patience has Matthew, now." There was a wistfulness in her tone, but no trace of envy. "And Tynan his Journey's End."

A fitting name, Rafe decided, for a ranch in the far reaches of Montana.

A trailing pelican squawked, begging for a treat. Then, squawking again in scolding disappointment, veered away to plunge beak first into the sea in search of its own meal.

Drawn from her reminiscence by the feathered indignation, Valentina hooked a careless thumb beneath the flimsy top, hitching it a scant inch higher over the sloping fullness it barely contained. Turning her undivided attention to Rafe, she drawled, "My, but you're talkative today."

Rafe smiled again. A smile that was amused and charming, as with smooth and practiced moves, he brought the sloop about in a wide, sweeping turn. "Just going with the flow."

"Just the flow, huh?"

"Something like that."

She nodded a noncommittal agreement, knowing that in his reticence he was carefully not pushing any more buttons before she was ready. Another sigh, long and grateful, and an inch regained was as heedlessly lost as the swimsuit top settled precariously lower. Lifting her gaze to the sky, she noted the altered angle of the sun. "Changing course?"

Rafe busied himself with the sail before answering casually. "Just making a small detour."

"Another detour, you mean."

"Do you mind?"

"I keep thinking there's somewhere you should be."

His answer was untroubled and thoughtful. "I'm exactly where I need to be, Valentina."

The words, as much as the slow look that skimmed over her, drew a glow of color to her cheeks. "McCallum International doesn't need its chief taskmaster?"

"If it does, I'm not the taskmaster I consider myself."

"A well-oiled machine, et cetera, et cetera?"

A minute adjustment, another minor shift in course and Rafe nodded. "Something like that."

Rising from the chaise, Valentina moved to the polished coaming that rimmed the sumptuously appointed sloop. Arms hugging her sides, rocking easily with the subtle buck of the vessel, she faced the oncoming shore and considered this man who had come into her life, taking her burdens as his, yet never intruding. He would be an exacting taskmaster, but fair and kind, never asking for more of another than he would give himself. It was no effort to imagine the loyalty and respect he would inspire among those with whom he dealt and worked. Nor that they would want to earn and keep his respect. As she did, at least for a little longer.

"So, Valentina, what shall it be?"

His quiet question, his musing tone, stroked her mind as subtly as his glance did her face and body as she turned to him. "What shall it be?"

"Detour?" With a gesture Rafe indicated the direction he'd abandoned. "Or return to course and full speed ahead to our final destination?"

Valentina didn't hesitate. In three days of sailing, in several meandering digressions along sweeping waterways, Rafe had shown her picturesque shorelines, quaint fishing villages and small but stately old shipping towns. One more could only lengthen their time together. "Detour." Sparing no thought for the transient truth that only days before she'd wanted nothing to do with Rafe, she smiled with interest in her eyes. "This one sounds special."

"It will be." He liked the way one brow lifted in a curious quirk and her eyes narrowed against the sun. "We have a dinner date."

"We do?" Hiding her surprise, she crossed the deck, halting a comfortable distance from him. "May I ask where, and with whom?"

"You'll see." Reaching out for her, Rafe drew her into the circle of his arms, keeping her willing prisoner as he steered in another wide, arcing turn from shore. A temporary abandonment of the course he'd just set. A natural digression.

Pleasant diversions in mind, kissing the top of her head as

his hand strayed to the vagabond top to aid and abet its wandering journey, he murmured, "Just not yet."

With sails furled and engine quiet, *The Summer Girl* drifted at anchor. Gulls wheeled and dipped curiously over the idle vessel, looking for a stray crumb. Lying in the shade afforded by a stretch of brightly striped canvas awning, Rafe never looked away from his self-appointed task of guarding Valentina's sleep. She rarely dreamed now, in fact never, but neither did he tire of watching her.

In the aftermath of their lovemaking, she was flushed and relaxed. Her lashes lay on her cheeks in a dark ruffle. Her mouth was soft and sultry from his kisses. An invitation he couldn't resist.

Bending to her, with his own mouth he traced the shape and angle of hers, knowing the instant she woke, feeling the curve of her smile beneath his. Drawing away a little he looked down at her. Her eyes were closed, her body languid. Only her naked breasts lifting in an uneven breath betrayed the quickening he saw in her smile. Her searching hand found his arm, sliding from there to his shoulder, his neck, his cheek. Fingers fluttered over his temple, clasped at his neck, tugging him gently down.

"More," she murmured as his lips were a breath away from hers. Her smile was wicked, the smile of a mischievous wanton as she flexed and stretched, brushing rose tipped breasts against the bareness of his chest.

"Shouldn't you open your eyes before you make that invitation?" Chuckling, Rafe turned his head into the cleft of her breasts, kissing the delicate slope of each. "Who knows who crept on board while you were sleeping. I might be a roving pirate, a seafaring warrior, or some fierce marauder come to ravish the beautiful maiden lying like a windflower on a beach sheet."

Lashes lifting only a trace, she regarded him drowsily through their dark veil. Her fingers strayed to his lips, gliding over them in erotic exploration. Her voice was husky, her look an invitation. "Aren't you?"

Green fire smoldered in the gaze that held hers. "Which would you say?"

"All." The word caught in her throat and her hips writhed against his as he nibbled at her fingers. "Definitely all."

"Which would you have, Valentina? Pirate? Warrior? Marauder?" With each name there was a caress. With each a promise. With each he tantalized and seduced. "When?"

Hardly aware of the heat of the sun or the wash of the sea, her body curled into his, scorched by a need no ocean breeze could ever cool. "You." Catching fistfuls of the gleaming black mane as it lay over his nape, she dragged his mouth again to her. "I would have you. Rafe Courtenay, pirate, warrior, marauder, I would have you now."

But as he took her arms from his neck, pinning her wrist by her shoulders on the beach sheet, Rafe had other intentions. He would be pirate, warrior and marauder. But more than that he would be her lover as never before.

Gazing down at her, he made no move to release her, letting his breath and the rise and fall of his chest tease the tightening bloom of her nipples. As the sensual caress drew a low moan from her, he shifted again, sliding his long brawny torso over her. Twining his legs through hers, he bent his head to offer comfort for the sweet anguish he'd created.

The lave of his tongue, the delicate suckle, sent sensations surging through her. Keening shafts of turmoil and need arched her body like a drawn bow as she sought more. When she would have struggled out of his grasp in her greed, he held her tighter, harder. Never ceasing in his own struggle of self-restraint, kissing, caressing with each move and shift of his body, he let the tide build.

Waiting and teasing. Teasing and waiting, he felt the growing hunger, the thirst, the lust. The bittersweet yearning. He felt its power, in him, in Valentina. And still he denied it. He touched, he stroked, he discovered. She trembled with each new exploration, and cried out in the anguish of incomplete ecstasy, needing him as much as he needed her.

And still he waited.

Loving her was always sweet, but this time would be all the sweeter for the wait. Wilder, fiercer, and more consummate for the aching pleasure of delay. This time he would take her to the brink of total destruction, when two people could survive only as one. That place where there was no sun, no moon, no walls. There, he would make her his. Only his.

Keeping himself from her, he plied his gentle torture, giving her every pleasure but the one she would have. With trembling heart and restraint of steel, he held back the ascending tide. As desperate as she, as needful, he endured.

Each time she bucked and lunged against him in mute cry that she could bear no more, with a kiss, the slide of his body, a worshiping suckle at her breasts, he took her deeper into the mania of desire and passion.

Abruptly, they were there, poised at the gate of nirvana, trembling at the fragile precipice of that perfect place only consummate lovers ever know. That wondrous, elusive place that once gained would not concede. Where there would be, or could be, no turning back. The culmination that could abide no longer than a heartbeat.

While the precipice crumbled away, he took her with him, at last, into the whirlpool of rapture.

As he released her wrists, freeing her, she reached out for him, grasping, clawing, bringing him to her and herself to him. Her mind and heart were frenzied, her skin feverish. The heat of her passion seared like a brand. Demanding. Commanding. Meeting passion with passion, branded and branding, Rafe lifted his body to hers, thrusting and driving into the embracing womanliness who trembled in need of him. Only for him.

Before, in their lovemaking, this moment had been couched in guarded care. Now that could not be, as shrouding walls tumbled and the final shred of reservation slipped from her.

There were no shadows between them, no reserve. She would be his, completely, as she had never been in all their lovemaking. And as he moved deeper, relentlessly, the intimate caress answering and soothing her most primitive longing, he was the pirate. The warrior. The marauder.

At last the fury that demanded release raged beyond any control. When it had ended, when in his heart and body and soul he had made her his, he watched her drowse again, replete in the afterglow. In that quiet time that follows the storm, he knew this was more than resolution of grief. More than proving she was worthy of life and love. More than anything he expected in all his life.

Musing and watching, while gulls continued their wheeling and dipping, while *The Summer Girl* drifted lazily at anchor, he knew in his mind what his heart had known all along...this was about love.

For love he had needed to make her his.

And as he guarded her dreams, for love, whoever he was, whatever he might become, he was hers.

Heart, body, and soul, she was a part of him. And he of her.

Rafe turned from his study of the marina and the Charleston skyline as he heard her footsteps on deck. Valentina stood poised at the top of the stairs, restless fingers toying with one of what appeared to be a hundred tiny silk-clad buttons marching down the length of her dress. From the modest decolletage, to the fluttering hem at her ankle, they winked and shimmered in the light, teasing him with the secrets hidden beyond their closure.

Crinkled pleats skimmed over her body, making promises of its wonders. Rich turquoise lay against her skin, flowing around her, lustrous as a gown of jewels. Her eyes, in contrast, were dark and unfathomable.

As she hesitated, heavy eyed and content, but uncertain after her reckless abandon, he wanted nothing as much as he wanted to take the dress from her slowly, teasing himself with the treasure each button revealed. But he knew himself and her effect well enough to know that one button and he would be lost. And there was not time.

Feasting his eyes on her, recalling the taste of sea spray on her skin, he committed to memory this sultry vision his love-making had created. When he would have made love to her beneath the stars and into the long sweet hours of the night, he must escort her ashore instead. His voice was hoarse with remembered passion, with secret and biding desire. "Ready?"

"Yes." Her hair had been slicked back from her forehead, then caught up in a single clip. Curls cascaded from her crown to her nape, with escaping strands brushing her throat and the top of her shoulders. Her slender neck was graceful and regal as she lifted her chin in familiar determination. Her look met his, keeping secrets of her own. "As ready as I will ever be."

Rafe offered his hand but did not touch her. With all her barriers torn asunder, Valentina was vulnerable as she'd never been. The first move, or any move must be hers.

Beneath the weight of her burning sapphire stare, he stood his ground. What he wanted and would have from her must come from strength and trust, not in a moment of fragility. With the wind ruffling and tugging at the pale linen slacks and dark silky shirt of his more formal attire, with light from the setting sun casting long shadows at his feet, he waited.

Letting her look stray from his to the long slender fingers he raised to her, Valentina understood this was much more than innate gallantry. The mood had changed between them. If she took the hand he offered, it would be more than the simple joining of hands. Her heart pounded in erratic rhythm, her mouth turned dry. Something inside her seemed to tremble, poised and yearning, needing him, needing his strength and his wisdom, but afraid.

Trust. From the deepest recesses of her heart and mind, the word threaded through her thoughts.

This was about trust and trusting. She had given him her body and reveled in the gift of his. Stepping beyond the walls of a lifetime, she'd gone with him into new worlds. Now he would have the rest, that secret part of her she had never shared with another soul. Could she bare the darkness of her spirit? Would he turn away from her when he knew?

This was about trust.

With no guarantees.

For either of them.

Meeting his attending gaze, as she probed the glittering green depths, she laid her fingers in his palm. "No guarantees."

His grip was hard and assuring. "We'll take it as it happens."

"What?" A word, a question, encompassing her fears and doubts.

"Whatever you wish. However you wish."

"Can it be that simple? That easy?"

"If we let it."

"How do we *let* anything happen?"

"By taking one day at a time." Drawing her to him, he tucked her hand through the crook of his arm, holding it closely against him. "By living each day to the fullest and accepting what it brings. No regrets, no recriminations."

"Pretending the past never existed?"

"No." Rafe sighed and clasped her arm closer. "By accepting the past as only that—the past. Perhaps part and parcel of what we've become, but finished."

Curls tumbled and shimmered as she turned her head in denial. "That can't be possible."

"It can be, and it is." His grasp was comforting, his smile slow and charming. "Tonight you'll see for yourself."

Valentina's brow lifted in speculation. "The mysterious dinner date, I suppose."

"Bingo!" Before she could react, or ask the myriad questions this bit of intrigue provoked, he guided her firmly to the ramp that led to the dock. "Watch and listen tonight. Then decide for yourself how the past and its tragedies have affected Jeb and Nicky. Find the harm the past has done their love, if you can."

Drawing Rafe to a halt with the pressure of her fingers, she turned to the view of Charleston Harbor. A tingle of surprise rushed through her as pieces of a puzzled fell into place. "Charleston," she murmured. "Jeb Tanner and Nicole Callison."

Rafe drew a long, gratified breath. He had gambled that within the secrecy of The Black Watch the legend of Jeb Tanner's prowess as an agent and his love for Nicole lived on. A secret shared, but honored and guarded.

"Jeb and Nicole Callison *Tanner*," he corrected quietly as the gamble was paid in recognition. Tucking her hand more securely over his arm, he walked with her to the boardwalk that linked the marina to land. The clack and creak of *The Summer Girl* bumping with the rhythm of the tide against her slip was lost in the hum of shore before he delivered the coup de grace. "They will be our host and hostess for the evening."

* * *

The marina teemed with seagoing vessels of every sort and size. Yachts, houseboats, sloops, runabouts and dinghies. Even a johnboat or two rocked jauntily with each current. But there was little sign of their inhabitants. An occasional laborer could be seen polishing and cleaning, or attending some minor chore. But for the most part, the small inlet and the natural harbor it formed seemed to laze in burgeoning radiance of the sultry southern climate, untouched by the bustle of an active port of call.

From its lazy peace to a spectacular view of historic waterways, it projected the ambience of another time, another era, even the most modern and sumptuous of its indigene could never dispel. Perhaps it was that mood that made it seem natural that a horse-drawn carriage should wait in a fluted edge of shade, bordering the grounds of the marina.

The carriage was a phaeton, the horses a pair of matched bays with the massive shoulders and fragile ankles of racers. The driver lounging against a wheel was a beautiful young man with skin like black satin. Catching sight of them, he pushed away from the carriage to approach them.

A dove gray cutaway hugged his wide shoulders and lay smoothly over his thick chest. A pin-striped, double-breasted vest buttoned snugly at his narrow waist. Creased and satin-banded trousers brushed spit-shined slippers, while a starched white shirt and a foulard with a ruby winking in its folds completed his accoutrements. Tall and massive, with the gliding, measured stride of a dancer, he moved over dusty track and uneven pavement. Yet with the acrid smells of gasoline and oil and diesel fuel wafting around him, neither he nor his carriage seemed truly out of place or time.

Intersecting their path, he stopped a pace away, doffing a meticulously blocked top hat and executing a sweeping bow. "Would you be going into the city, sir?"

His voice was a rich bass rising from the deep well of his chest. Soft and cultured, there lurked a hint of merriment in it. But when he straightened, his bearing that of kings, his face was blandly expressionless. From this proximity, Valentina could see that silver tinged his temples and glittered here and there among dark, tight curls. A look of maturity and confidence marked his face, though the only lines were faint crinkles fanning from the corner of his eyes. Laugh lines, yet his gaze was grave.

With her arm pressed against Rafe's side, and her fingertips lying at his wrist, she felt the leap of his pulse as he nodded his answer.

"Then perhaps you would choose to go in style. See the city as it should be seen. Hear a little of its history." A gentle sales pitch, delivered with the panache of one who had done it countless times.

"I know the history of Charleston," Rafe said bluntly.

"Ahh, perhaps you do, sir. But not as I would tell it." Something like hidden laughter lurked in the softly accented tone.

Sensing more than the casual encounter merited, Valentina looked from one handsome man to the other. A little perplexed, keeping her own counsel and her silence, she waited and observed.

"Put your own spin on history, do you?" Rafe suggested more than asked.

"I prefer to call it factual narrative embellished with a touch of speculation and imagination for the enjoyment of my fares." Almost as an afterthought the driver added, "Enlightenment and entertainment, sir."

"And if I want neither enlightenment nor entertainment, why should I chose to ride in your carriage?"

"Because there's no place more romantic than Charleston in the moonlight."

"The sun is shining," Rafe drawled wryly.

"Yes, sir, I believe it is." The top hat was set at a rakish angle, the brim drawn down over his forehead. "But the day passes quickly."

"While I keep you waiting and in need of a fare."

"Exactly."

"May I suppose that the need for a fare is what has you ranging so far afield, away from the city proper?"

A shrug lifted the shoulders of the gray cutaway. "Fares are dollars and cents, and you may think and suppose whatever you like. But you are in need of a ride, are you not?"

Valentina turned her gaze, again, from one man to the other. The strange conversation rivaled a tennis match, with each player serving zinging aces, one after the other. A curious gull swooped and curled, a darting shadow falling over them. Neither Rafe nor the driver noticed.

"We need a ride," Rafe spoke again in the long, slow drawl. "But what if I'm not interested in moonlight and romance?"

"Then, sir," the cultured tone, the perfect diction became a drawl mimicking Rafe's, "with Miss O'Hara on your arm, I'd call you one helluva fool."

Valentina smothered a gasp, surprised that a stranger knew her name, that he would speak as he did to prospective fares he needed.

Rafe showed no sign of sharing her surprise. "A fool, huh?"

"In spades."

"I couldn't agree more." Then Rafe was releasing her, stepping away, his hand extended. "Jase." The greeting became a long inspection from arm's length, then an embrace, toppling the hat in the dust.

Backing away, the men smiled, then grinned, then laughed. Valentina was forgotten.

"Good Lord." Rafe shook his head. "How long has it been?"

"Too long," the man called Jase declared. "But I can see time's been good to you."

"And to you. Miranda! How is she?"

"Randy's fine. Finer than fine."

"She's in Paris? A buying trip for her store?"

"She *was* in Paris."

"Until she heard about Jordana, and then she was on her way home, immediately," Rafe suggested.

Jase laughed. "She would have been. Sooner than immediately, but there was a hitch. The airport was fogged in. All flights delayed. I thought she was going to start walking home."

Rafe remembered the days before Jordana's marriage to Patrick, when Miranda had been her companion, her friend, her eyes. "But she's with Jordana now?"

"Has a cat got a tail? Is the sky blue? Are we being rude to your lady?"

"Yes, we are," Rafe acknowledged. "But not for a moment longer." Turning, taking her hand, he drew Valentina to him, and a circle of two became three.

"Miss O'Hara, Mr. Boone. Jason, Valentina." The introduction accomplished, Rafe drew her closer, murmuring sotto voce, "Don't be fooled by the act or the patter. Jason Boone owns a fleet of carriages and a stable of the most beautiful horses ever to work in harness. He needs more fares about as much as he needs another wife."

Jase rolled his eyes and grinned again. "I thank God every day that Hattie Boone took me into her life, and that through her I met Patrick and Jordana, and Randy. But believe me, Randy Taylor is all the wife I want, or would ever want." His grin widened. "To tell the truth, brother, she's all I can handle."

Rafe laughed at that, agreeing with a twinkle in his eyes. "Be careful, Jase. Your bride of...how many years?"

"Three," Jase provided. "Three fiery, unpredictable, wonderful years."

"Your bride of three fiery, unpredictable, wonderful years, once promised Patrick she would cut his heart out."

"Only if he hurt Jordana deliberately," the dark man interjected. "Be assured the same rule applies to any man or woman, when it comes to Cassie."

"And Courtney." Rafe put in. Bringing Valentina another inch closer, sweeping a clinging ebony tendril from her face, he said softly, "This time, for Courtney, thank God there was O'Hara."

"Indeed." Jase turned a beaming gaze toward her, his eyes thoughtful, almost purple in their darkness.

Hattie, Miranda, Cassie. The names rang in Valentina's mind. She felt oddly detached, disoriented, as if she'd come into the middle of a story, with characters she'd yet to meet, but should know.

"Rafe," Jase scolded. "What are we thinking? A poor example of Southern gentlemen we are! Keeping your lady standing in the sun and the dust, while we reminisce about old times and old friends. You have a couple of hours before your dinner engagement, the least we can do is show her the city. If we move along with it, that should save a half hour for the pièce de résistance. In the interim, if she's interested, we can explain who's on first.''

The remark left her blinking, wondering what baseball had to do with anyone and anything.

Catching sight of her perplexity, Rafe chuckled and led her to the carriage. "When you know Jase better, you'll learn that the best comedy team that ever lived, in his estimation, was Abbott and Costello.''

"Who's on first? I don't know!" Valentina recalled the routine that was her father's favorite. "I don't know know's on…" Laughing she cut short her recitation from the movie *The Naughty Nineties*. The very best of Bud Abbott and Lou Costello.

Laughter drifted over the marina as Rafe helped her to the burnished leather of the phaeton's seats. One look convinced her this was a carriage for special occasions, never making the rounds of Charleston's narrow streets filled with visitors. Another mark of the respect and friendship she perceived.

Then Rafe was beside her, his hip and thigh brushing hers in close quarters, and she thought only of him.

After a deft check of horses and harnessing, as he swung into the driver's seat and took up his whip, Jason Boone glanced over his shoulder. "Rafe, my man, none of us was taking bets that you'd ever settle down. But I think you've found the one. As smart as she is talented. Brave as she is beautiful—and she knows Abbott and Costello. Lord, man, she's perfect. Don't let her get away.''

The whip sang in the air, matched bays leapt into a steady trot. While Jase guided them from the marina to a street that would lead to the city, Rafe laced his fingers through Valentina's and settled back, anticipating the rest of the show. As the countryside changed and the trappings of the city grew more frequent, he muttered only to himself, "Let O'Hara get away? Not if I can stop her.''

In a fraction less than an hour and a half, when he brought the team and carriage to a halt at the entrance of a narrow cul-de-sac, Jason Boone was as good as his word. Valentina had seen the city as never before, and learned that Hattie Boone was Jase's adoptive mother and caretaker of Eden, Patrick McCallum's island paradise. She knew that before Randy Taylor became Jase's wife, she had been a bit of everything for Jordana, but a friend most of all. Cassie, Randy's daughter, was more than Jase's stepdaughter, she was the light of his soul.

"That's it, kiddies—*the tour*." Jase put away the tasseled whip and turned in his seat. "Next visit, there'll be more. The really special stuff." With a check of his watch, a grin, and a theatrical gesture, he announced, "And now, the pièce de résistance, Callison Gallery."

Looking in the direction he indicated, Valentina saw a row of tiny shops, each with windows displaying its ware. Boutiques, antiques, candies, candles, and clothing. It was a pretty little side street of quaint storefronts and walled courtyards, ending at the door of dark wood and leaded glass, bearing the name of the gallery and its hours in discreet, curling script.

"Be warned, Valentina, a half hour won't be nearly enough, and you'll be tempted to linger. But, unless you want to play at being dreadfully Charlestonian and arrive fashionably late at the Tanners'..."

"We'll be here, Jase," Rafe promised. "At the appointed time."

"Your chariot and its driver will be waiting."

The street was as lovely and quaint up close as from a distance. The door to the gallery as subdued and classically elegant. As it swung open on well oiled hinges, a bell announced their arrival.

"Hello," a cheerful voice called from the nether regions of the shop. "Make yourselves at home and I'll be with you shortly."

Almost before she finished speaking, before Valentina could take in the astonishing works of art scattered throughout the gallery, a woman hardly taller than a child came rushing to them.

"Rafe!" As portly as she was beautiful, the laughing bundle of energy launched herself into his arms. "You handsome devil! Where have you been for so long? And why did it take a near tragedy to bring you back to us?"

Not waiting for an answer, turning like a whirlwind, she

faced Valentina. "And you!" she declared vehemently, tilting her head, studying the taller woman thoughtfully. "We've heard so many wonderful things about you. How can we ever thank you?"

"O'Hara, you've just met Annabelle Devereaux," Rafe explained with a chuckle.

"Of course she has." The copper-hued planes of Annabelle's face curved into a smile. A Gypsy's black mane fairly trembled in her delight. "Come," she offered Valentina a hand with magenta nails. "We'll get better acquainted while I give you the fifty-cent safari through the gallery."

With Annabelle chattering like a knowledgeable magpie and Rafe trailing behind, Valentina found the gallery fascinating. Nicole Callison Tanner had amassed an astonishing array of work, with each uniquely exhibited. An unintentional expression of her own talents.

"So," Annabelle finished with a flourish. "If you had to choose, which would be your favorite?"

Valentina turned slowly, reviewing the exhibits. "It would be difficult to choose."

"Jeb likes the wolf. Nicky, anything by Ashley Blackmon. And Rafe," Annabelle's fond glance swept over him, "everything and anything by Hunter Slade."

"Indeed," Valentina agreed, remembering the strong but innately lovely sculptures that were Hunter Slade's. *"Freedom,"* she said turning to a small bronze replica of a woman, her gown and long hair forever flying in an eternal wind, her arm raised to the sky, a seahawk lifting from her open palm. "I've never seen anything lovelier or more exhilarating than *Freedom.*"

"You've chosen my favorite, as well." Enveloping Valentina in her bosomy embrace, Annabelle kissed her cheek. "I'm glad you've come and I hope you'll become one of us."

Before Valentina could respond, the little woman was spinning to Rafe, including him in her affections. "Much as I'd like you to stay, you'd better hurry along. Nicky has a wonderful dinner planned. It would be a shame to be late."

Valentina was quiet as the door closed behind them, silencing the soft ring of the bell. With Rafe by her side, the day had been marvelous and full. An exciting adventure, leaving her with much to consider, much to think on.

In the hush of twilight, their footsteps sounded in cadence on ancient brick pavers. At the end of the darkening street, Jase and his chariot waited.

Ten

"Almost there, now," Jase announced, his singsong bass a ripple in the silent restraint pervading the carriage.

Lamps from another century lined the narrow side street as he turned the horses into it. Iron-clad wheels trundled over uneven pavement, leaving the marvelous mansions of Charleston and The Battery, with waves of a tranquil sea washing endlessly against its protecting walls, behind.

On this route rarely traveled by carriages for hire, beneath the massive branches of an avenue of oaks, houses constructed on a scale far less grand marched in imperfect lines. In the quaintly repetitious style unique to Charleston, each differed only in the mark of the personalities and distinctive individuality of those who lived and played, sequestered within their bounds.

The home that had once been a *pied-à-terre* for Nicole Callison on days when business at the gallery kept her late in the city was no different, and no less exceptional. The same ingenious talent that made the gallery riveting and exciting had transformed it from temporary lodgings to a home possessed of welcoming grace and comfortable charm.

But as Jase called a soft good evening, and the horses clopped slowly away, neither welcoming grace nor comfortable charm could quiet the anxious flutters in Valentina's throat.

"Nervous?" Rafe asked quietly in her ear, the heat of his body touching her, reassuring her.

"Some," she admitted. "Jeb Tanner is a man of heroic achievements, an example given to all of us. I never expected to meet him." That fledgling recruits who followed in Jeb's footsteps were in awe of him was quite the truth. But not the total reason for Valentina's malaise. In her travels with her family she'd met the great and near great often enough to be skilled and practiced in whatever protocol or formality each required. But these were Rafe's friends. People to whom he was special, and were special to him. It was that, as much as Jeb Tanner's celebrity among the clandestine Watch, that caused her disquiet.

"Don't get cold feet on me now. You passed Jase's inspection, and Annabelle's. And, believe it, she's one tough lady. Sure, Jeb's all you've been taught he is, and all you've heard. Even more. But when the last is said and done, he's simply a man. As Nicky, for all her talents and her strengths, is simply a woman. You'll like them both, I promise."

Biting her lip, Valentina held back a tremor and tried for a smile. "The question is, will they like me?"

"That, my love, is guaranteed." Rafe smiled back at her. In this vulnerable moment, with the endearment shimmering in the night between them, he ached to take her in his arms and hold her. But Jeb and Nicole were waiting, and the moment passed. Taking her hand to forestall any more angst and delay, without ringing or knocking, with the assurance of one who had visited many times, he led her from the street.

Beyond delicately ornate gates of iron, lay a courtyard and garden, exquisitely planned, meticulously tended. The night was humid and heavy with the fragrance of flowers scattered along ancient walls and patterned walks. The glow of a coach lamp fell on waxy leaves of evergreens, painting them with the patina of antique velvet. In this rectangular corridor of garden and lawn, Charleston stepped firmly back into the past, becoming a magical place of stately gentility and quiet majesty. The perfect setting for the lovely woman who rushed across the veranda to greet them.

"Valentina." From the flowing sleeves of a gown that was the summation of understated, casual chic, the hands of a gardener reached out to her. Their strong grip belying the fragile elegance both the gown and Nicky Tanner projected. "I'm so glad you could come, I've hoped so much that someday we could meet. We're sure to be friends." A mischievous smile swept from Rafe to Jeb. "With so much in common, and considering that the ever elusive Rafe Courtenay is so smitten he would bring you to dinner, how could we not?"

Letting a laughing Jeb and a smiling but quiet Rafe trail in her wake, Nicky swept Valentina into the house and to dinner.

Dinner was a pleasant affair, complete with silver and china and crystal and lace. The table was small and intimate and complemented by lively conversation. There was never a hint of the stilted reserve Valentina expected as an outsider. Though the certainty of Nicky's logic escaped her, Valentina did, indeed, feel that she and her vivacious hostess might have been friends.

Jeb was quieter, but no less genial, and obviously deeply in love with his wife.

After a meal of low country delicacies, over coffee and dessert, conversation turned to old times and old acquaintances. The list read like who's who in Valentina's world. Some she knew, some she'd only heard of, some not even that. And though The Black Watch was never mentioned, all of them seemed interconnected. Part of a far-ranging brotherhood, if not The Watch, itself.

Even Rafe.

As she watched him from her place across the table, she wondered how a "civilian" had become and remained closely tied with an organization so cautiously circumspect. She wondered, but did not ask, filing her questions away for another time as conversation rippled and eddied, moving swiftly over a variety of subjects.

"Jase tells us Jordana is recovering so miraculously that Randy will be coming home soon." Jeb set down his empty wineglass and pushed it away. "We spent an evening with

Patrick and Jordana during the Games at Grandfather recently.''

"Jeb speaks of the Highland Games," Nicky interpreted in an aside for Valentina's benefit. "Grandfather is a mountain in North Carolina, not a man." Then, answering questions she could only surmise Valentina must wonder about, she clarified and elaborated. "I would imagine you know, or have heard, the Scottish Games are Simon's favorite spectator sport. Perhaps you don't know they are often fertile ground for recruiting." With dark, winged brows lifting beneath the bangs of her short-cropped mane, she added, drolly, "Recruiting of one sort or another.

"Understanding that, and his love for the games, it shouldn't come as any surprise that Simon met Patrick there long ago. And as night follows day, through Patrick, he met Rafe. Over the years they've shared both friendships and adventures. Each calling on the other in time of need...as friends should."

Jeb flashed a smile of apology at Valentina for his oblique reference. Another of fond gratitude at Nicky for the explanation. "In any case," he continued, "the McCallum clan is a beautiful family. It would be tragic if anything happened to them."

"But nothing did." Stroking Valentina's cheek, then the path of a curl that drifted to her shoulder, Rafe assured, "Nothing Courtney can't deal with."

Into a thoughtful moment, while a rush of color subsided from Valentina's throat and cheeks, in the manner of a considerate and accomplished hostess, Nicky blithely announced a tidbit of good news. "Cassie will be studying art with a private instructor after Thanksgiving."

"Will she, now?" Taking his hand from Valentina's shoulder, Rafe chuckled, remembering gaudy pictures of an elephant called Humphrey taped to a refrigerator door in Jordana's kitchen. "Her talent was evident years ago."

On that remark, discussion turned to lighter and far ranging subjects.

As the pleasant evening drew near its end, when the last drop of coffee had been drunk and the last sliver of pecan pie put away, Nicole issued Rafe an invitation he couldn't refuse.

While the two of them cleared the table and retreated to the kitchen in a rush of delighted banter, Jeb volunteered for what he deemed the pleasure of showing Valentina the garden.

"Shall we, my dear?" he asked with a bow as courtly as any gentleman from any century who might have ever lived in his home. "The garden is nearing the end of its best blooming season, but it's still quite pleasant."

"I imagine it's always so," Valentina replied with the same old-fashioned decorum as she accepted his invitation.

Leaving laughter and conversation behind, they walked together in the moonlight, with Jeb letting her wander as she would and he only a half pace behind. In a subtle shift of moods, in a natural closing of ranks, they were the old guard and the new. Simon's chosen.

Sights and sounds of the Southern city were locked far away beyond thick, towering walls. The world, for a little while, was this lush garden. There was no small talk between them. No narration identifying and explaining this flower or that. Jeb simply strolled with her through the paths, letting her reflect and absorb and, perhaps, share its peace.

Their footsteps were slow and meandering, and almost soundless. Only the oaks whispered in a random breeze. A natural accompaniment for the splash and burble of a miniature fountain.

"A penny," Jeb spoke as she halted by the glittering fall, tumbling into a small pool.

"I beg your pardon?" Valentina turned to him, not quite certain what he'd said, or what he meant.

"I offered you a penny." The man of legend answered gently, a penny lying in the hollow of his palm. "To make a wish."

"Then this is a wishing well."

Tall and dark, with eyes as silver as the moon, Jeb nodded. With the composure that marked the man he'd been, the man he was, he watched as she tossed the penny and bowed her head.

The muted sound of the splash had faded, the ripples disappeared, before she moved away.

As calmly as he'd waited, as thoughtfully as he'd observed, Jeb bridged a chasm of silence. "Nicky says the fountain must be a wishing well, for it's a wish come true. Something she always wanted, to make the garden complete." He trailed a fingertip over weathered coping and, catching up a flower at its edge, scattered tender petals like crimson snowflakes over reflected moonlight. "It was my gift to her when we were married."

A wonderfully romantic thought that once she would have considered quite out of character. "You knew she wanted it?"

"No." Those who had called him rigid and saturnine, the dedicated, disciplined hunter, would not now. There was a softness in him. Tenderness. "It seemed..." he paused, searching for the word, choosing the simplest. "It seemed right."

Valentina nodded. Some things needed no more explanation.

"Come." Jeb offered a hand callused with the rigors of the labors of his new life. "Let me show you our favorite place."

As she went with him, her hand in his, Valentina recalled a rumor whispered among The Black Watch. Jeb Tanner, manhunter without peer, had traded "spyhood" for apron strings and a hammer. Over dinner, when the conversation had turned from people and distant places and moved closer home, in bits and pieces she learned he had become expert in the rescue and restoration of some of Charleston's oldest buildings. If his intuition and the rightness of his choice of the fountain was any indication, then, she decided, he must be even more brilliant in his second profession.

As she mused over gossip and fact, he led her toward a far corner, to a park bench. A relic from another era in flawless repair. One, she suspected, rescued and restored by Jeb to enhance and complete this favored space. From her seat beneath gnarled branches of a crape myrtle as venerable, her view encompassed the whole of the garden. And with it, the worn service walk, then the gate shutting away the traffic of the street. The latter, flanked by cloistering shrubs, shielding the softly lighted windows of the tiny, but elegant Charleston single. The haven Jeb and Nicole Tanner called home.

For a moment she was contented there in the shadows, the silent man at her side. For a moment she could suspend thought and doubt, believing in wishes in the peaceful refuge two lovers had created.

But reality could never be far away, and never truly forgotten.

It was Jeb who spoke of it first. Taking her hand, he folded it in both of his as he turned her to face him. "There's something you need to ask me, isn't there, Valentina?"

There it was. Straight for the jugular, no matter how kindly asked, as the Jeb Tanner of old would do.

Drawn from a pensive reverie, for the space of a fleeting frown she was bewildered, her thoughts scattered. Then her heart plummeted. "This is about David. Rafe told you. That's why he brought me here, to force the issue. That's what this little walk in the garden is all about, isn't it?"

"No, my dear, it isn't. And you're wrong on every count. What Rafe has told us of you had nothing to do with David. Neither you nor I can deny that in many tragic ways our lives parallel each other, but that's simply ironic coincidence and nothing to do with his purpose. Rafe brought you here to give you the chance to witness for yourself that there is and can be life after The Black Watch." Squeezing her hand gently, he assured her, "There is no other reason, Valentina."

She wanted to believe as Jeb did. Her need to believe was written on her face. "How can you be so certain?"

"Rafe, and the sort of man he is, is my certainty. Granted, he knows you and David were partners, members of the same police force, the same SWAT team. He knows David died in the line of duty. And he knows you were involved in some way. He wouldn't be human if he hadn't drawn his own conclusions from the dreams. But even they had nothing to do with this evening."

Jeb grinned, then, not in humor, but self-deprecation. "You realize, I hope, that all of this is sheer supposition and deduction drawn from my great trove of wisdom. But, to reiterate the important point, Rafe has said nothing."

Tilting her head slowly from side to side, Valentina muttered, "Then how?"

"How do I know?" The grin became a grimace. "The same way you know my history, I imagine."

That she knew was an assumption, never a question. "The grapevine," she acknowledged. "Of course."

"Of course." Jeb sighed. "A cliché, but a fact. For a super-secret organization, little is truly secret within the bounds of The Black Watch. While I may not take an active part any longer, I'm not completely out of touch. I have my contacts and another particularly reliable source, as well."

"Simon!" she blurted.

"Naturally." The admission was swiftly qualified. "But only because he was concerned about you and thought I would understand better than most."

"Then you know more than the grapevine could ever supply. You know what I did." Valentina was unaware that her nails scored the back of his hand, leaving marks that would be no little time in fading. "You know what I couldn't do."

"I know."

Dragging in a shuddering breath, she asked the question he had anticipated from the first. "Could you? Years ago, when a madman held a gun to Nicole's head, if your partner hadn't been there, what would you have done?"

Jeb went still, considering, weighing. Affording her query the soul searching it merited. When he spoke, his voice was strong, ringing with conviction. "Could I have shot Tony Callison, even when he had been my best friend?" Pausing, his head inclined once, abruptly. "The answer is, yes.

"Could I have shot him knowing that no matter what he'd become, Tony was still Nicky's brother?" His hand was hard and steady over Valentina's. "Yes. For what he had done, for what he might do, unequivocally, yes!

"But could I have fired a shot with the knowledge that if my aim veered off target by even an inch it would be my bullet that killed Nicole?"

Releasing her, Jeb stood up to pace. The tranquility of the garden was suddenly effaced. A hand at his nape kneaded taut muscles. Turning, he stared at moving figures silhouetted against the dining room window. One was Nicole, vibrant and alive, and safe. Thanks to Mitch Ryan, more than Jeb Tanner.

The scene that had played thousands of times through his mind in flashing vignettes was as vivid tonight as then. The players as real as if they stood before him now.

Nicole and the hulking man-child, Ashley Blakemond. Innocent hostages.

Mitch Ryan, Matthew Winter Sky. His partners, men of The Black Watch.

And Tony Callison. Friend, brother. Killer of children.

A struggle.

Gunshots. Tony's Mitch's.

Blood. Everywhere, blood.

One Callison died.

One lived.

"Nicole."

Jeb watched her move beyond the windows, he heard the drift of her laughter. Bowing his head, he studied the ground as if the grass kept the secret of his quandary. After a while, he straightened, his gaze returning to the windows. His voice was only a husk of itself. "Would I have taken that shot?"

Callused hands clenched into fists. Distended veins throbbed beneath the upturned sleeve of his shirt. "I don't know. God help me! I don't know."

Valentina felt his hurt, the painful indecision. She had lived it. Yet, she had to ask, "Even after all these years?"

Wheeling away from his view of the windows, he looked long and hard at his troubled guest. No matter that she needed and wanted it, there was no pat response. "If I live to be a hundred I won't know, Valentina."

"If there had been no one else, if you'd had no choice..."

"Would I have hesitated?" Moving to her, with a knuckle at her chin he raised her dark gaze to his. "Wouldn't anyone?"

"I don't." Her tone was without inflection, lifeless. "Not now. Not anymore."

"Quick-draw O'Hara? Shoot without a thought or a qualm?" Jeb paused, drew a long considering breath. "I don't think so," he said with utter conviction. "Only when there's no other choice."

"A deduction drawn from your great trove of wisdom, I suppose." There was no rancor in her remark.

"Better than that. Proven fact."

"You speak of Courtney McCallum."

"For her sake, you waited. And you were right to wait."

"This time."

"Perhaps every time," Jeb suggested. "I suspect, especially with David."

"What you suspect and change will buy a cup of coffee."

A small smile ghosted over his mouth for only a second before his handsome features turned somber once more. "Let it go, O'Hara."

It was chance that he chose that moment to use one of Rafe's favorite names for her. But it got her attention, made her listen, shaking her to her toes.

"Let it go, dammit. You took a monster's life to save a child. When it was your lover, you couldn't. Not the same circumstances, I suspect not even the same woman, but the outcome is still the same. Nothing can change that. *Nothing!* So, accept it, learn from it, live with it." He grasped her cheeks between thumb and forefinger, cradling her chin in his palm, refusing to let her look away. "*Live.* Not even David Flynn would want you to crawl in the grave with him."

"You never knew David. You can't know what he would want."

"If he loved you, if he was worthy of your love, I know."

"Worthy!" For the first time, a flare of anger turned her tone harsh and grating. An alien sound at odds with what the garden should be. "Ahh, the voice of wisdom again. Tell me more."

"Not I." As he backed away, the clipped tone eased in compassion. "I have two questions, then you tell yourself."

"Only two?" Her face was grave, her mood sinking again into empty weariness as brief anger seeped out of her.

Jeb held up his hand, palm toward her, the mark of a new life, a new profession, slick and shining in the light. In a gesture reminiscent of Simon, he folded his fingers into his palms, stopping short of a perfect fist. "Two, I promise."

"Fine."

"You were in love with David?"

"Yes." Blunt, definitive. No qualifications. An unintentional revelation of the depth of her pain.

Though he hated what he'd heard and what he'd done, Jeb knew there was no other way to make her see. She had come into his home a stranger, someone he knew and who knew him by reputation alone. But they had shared too much the same to remain strangers. He hoped that now he could make her face and understand what he'd had to face and understand himself.

"My second question, and the last, is of the sort I asked myself. A search of my heart and a truthful answer resolved my difficulty." Kneeling before her, he took her clasped hands in his. "If the circumstances were reversed, if you had been taken hostage that day, if it were you who died, maybe for a moment of hesitation, maybe not, what would you want for David?"

He heard a stifled groan of regret, he felt her tense. Before she could speak, he released her and patted her knee. "Give it some time before you answer. Weigh the options and what you've been through and put yourself through. Then think of it in terms of David and what you would want for him. Think hard. Think long. Give it a week, two. A month. However long it takes. But, in the end, be honest, Valentina."

There was an expression of surprise on her face, and when she looked at him at last, he saw the glitter of unshed tears on her lashes. With the brush of his fingertips he wiped them away.

"Yes, David died. Nothing you can do or say, or deny yourself, can ever change that." His tone was compassionate, yet firm. "But many have lived, perhaps because of him. Remember. Take your time. Think."

Rising, he stood looking down at her. "And now it's my time to think, and what I think is that what you need more than anything right now is a good man to hold you. Just to share his strength. No demands made, no questions asked." He smiled then, the fond smile of a brother, or an uncle, or an instant friend. "I know the perfect man for the job. We both do.

"It can work out if you'll let it. Trust yourself, O'Hara. Trust him." Jeb's voice grew deeper, quieter, roughening in a gruff whisper. "Remember this, as well, even wishes that are possible can only come true if we let them."

He touched her cheek, a parting gesture. "Trust."

In half a minute he disappeared into the shadows of low

hanging limbs. In another she heard his footstep crossing the veranda.

The door opened and closed once.

And again.

Then it was Rafe who emerged from the same shadows.

Rafe who slipped into the seat beside her.

Rafe who held her in his arms, asking nothing, requiring nothing, saying simply, "I'm here, O'Hara. For as long as you need me."

As she tensed subtly, a chaotic cry constricting her throat, he sighed but didn't release her. Kissing the top of her hair, filling himself with her fragrance, he held her as he would've held Courtney when the troubles of her world were too much.

"I'm here," he promised again. "For as long as you want me."

Valentina huddled in his arms. Her mind and heart in turmoil, her body grateful for his embrace.

From the street there was the clatter of a horsedrawn carriage. The soft song of its driver. Jase, come to take them away from this enchanted place that was, per chance, her Armageddon.

Within the walls of the garden a night-bird swooped by on dark wings. Water splashed and danced—a lover's gift, glittering like fallen moonlight. Bright copper pennies bearing wishes gleamed in a pool of hope.

Trust. Truth.

Without one, the second could not be.

Wishes. Hope.

Need. A man for a woman. A woman for a man.

A dream. Only a dream.

Just for this moment, in this magical place, it had all seemed so clear. So easy. But now, beyond the sheltering walls, Jase waited with his chariot, to take them back to the real world.

Clouds that seemed to rise out of the water hovered against the horizon. A warning.

A storm brewed at sea.

Born as a summer squall, it had moved in fits and starts. Winding, zigging, then zagging. An unpredictable, recalcitrant,

Neptunian child of nature, sweeping over the open sea, gathering up its moisture, growing heavy and fecund. Then stalling, at last. A mutant seed, seething, spawning, gorging on its young, sucking more and more into its maw. In murky striations of black upon black, monstrous cells of waiting violence rose in a curiously blank faced wall to the sky.

The sea before the hovering storm was oily and torpid. The air eerily still, as if the world were becalmed and holding its breath.

Sails furled and hatches battened, her engines laboring, *The Summer Girl* plowed through glassy doldrums. Casting another of many worried looks at the sky, Rafe gripped Valentina's shoulder. "I need to go below to catch the next weather report. Can you manage?"

Laying her hand over his, she touched him for the first time since they'd said goodbye to Jeb and Nicole and, finally, to Jase. Her night aboard the sloop had been sleepless, the space Rafe had given her worse than lonely. Welcoming the morning, she rejoiced in returning to the mind-numbing rigors of the open sea. Now she would contend with what each brought. "I'll be fine. The storm is far enough away that we'll have at least some warning when it begins to move."

"Let's hope we get lucky and it doesn't move this way."

"My fingers are crossed."

"If our luck runs out, there's a chance we can make the island before it hits." Taking his hand from her shoulder, he glanced again at the sky. "An hour," he grumbled. "With the engines at top speed, that's all we need."

Leaving the sloop under her command, he went below, and Valentina was alone, surrounded by the empty sea and the prickling foreboding of the storm.

Like the good ship she was, *The Summer Girl* needed little attention in calm seas. With only minor adjustments to keep her course, and nothing else to do, time dragged by. Long seconds stretched into longer minutes. From a patch of incongruously blue sky, heat fell like an anvil. Hammering at Valentina, sucking moisture from her as the impending gale had from the sea. Sweat beaded her forehead and trickled in her eyes. Her white shirt was soaked and plastered to her body.

The band of her cutoffs had grown stiff with salt, chafing the tender skin at her waist.

Fully cognizant of the danger, she was oddly grateful for the heat and discomfort, and the mind-numbing drag of time. For a little while she didn't have to think or feel or face the challenge Jeb Tanner had given her.

Warning this respite was only temporary and drawing quickly to an end, lightning flashed against the horizon and thunder rolled over the sea. The first hint of wind stirred the air, and a choppy wave rocked the sloop. Before the sea had settled again to the glassy calm, Rafe was there, by Valentina's side, taking the wheel from her.

"The storm is moving again. By all reports it's coming this way. We have two choices, batten down and ride out the worst, or make a run for the island. One is as good or bad as the other." Rafe faced her squarely. "If we stay, we could be swamped. If we run for it, it will have to be a team effort, each of us working with the other. Trusting the other.

"It's your choice, sweetheart," he said with a peculiar lack of inflection. "We do as you say."

Her choice—a decision that could mean both their lives. Not a test. Trust.

She couldn't turn away from it. As he had, she scanned the sky, probing the secrets of the storm, anticipating, judging. "We go," she said at last, accepting his trust.

"Good." Rafe's smile was an exhilarated flash of white in his weather-beaten face. "That's my lady."

Now time that had dragged sped by. Even as they readied for their ordeal, tearing free of its doldrums, the seething storm swept along the water's surface. The wind whispered about them, then moaned, then howled. The sky darkened, the last of blue obscured. Rain like pelting stones began to fall in gusting sheets.

Neither Rafe nor Valentina had time to notice the stinging hurt nor did they care. As *The Summer Girl* ran before the wind, her bow sometimes dipping beneath the surface of the water, sometimes rearing far above it, keeping their course and staying aboard became the primary concern.

When he shielded her, taking the brunt of a wave that knocked him off his feet and sent him headlong into the path of the swinging boom, Valentina was there to take the wheel and help him to his feet. Fear for him lent her incredible strength even as it clenched like a vise in her breast.

"You're hurt," she cried out her alarm, as his blood mixed with rain and dripped from his forehead and face to his soaked shirt.

"Just a scratch. Head wounds bleed profusely, and it looks like more than it is because of the water." Raking an arm across his face he struggled to clear his vision. He made light of his fall, but his moves were deliberate, his tongue clumsy and his eyes glassy from the stunning blow.

"Sure," she agreed for the sake of avoiding an argument, with the wind snatching the words from her lips. "Only a scratch. But just in case..." Letting her actions finish for her, she wrapped a length of rope around his waist, then her own and, finally, the base of the helm. Securely anchored, taking the knife belted at her hip, she slashed at the hem of her shirt, ripping and tearing as she fought to keep her balance and their course.

"We have to keep going, stay ahead," he managed, sweeping blood and saltwater from his blinded eyes again. "Rough as this is, there's worse behind it."

"We will," she vowed with a desperate determination. "This was my decision and I won't betray a trust again."

Returning the knife to its sheath, and risking taking her hands from the wheel, she grasped his wrists, guiding his hands to grip where hers had been. He was groggy, but instinct and the strength of desperation were still there, in his arms, in his hands. "Hold it," she shouted against his ear to keep the sound from being lost to the wind.

"Just like this." She curled his fingers tighter around the wheel. "Just for a minute."

He didn't respond, but she felt the muscles flex as he took control of the sloop. As quickly as she could, she looped the ragged length of shirttail around his forehead, tying it tightly to guard the wound and hold back the flow of blood.

The contrast of ragged, jagged white angled over his darkened skin and the soaked black cap of his hair was startling. And no less so when it began to stain with scarlet. He could easily have been the thief or the pirate of his teasing lovemaking. As she stared at him, nerves still taut and keening with the sudden surge of alarm, she suspected he was all in one—the one who had captured her heart.

Fear for him made her realize how much she cared. How much she wished dreams tossed into a pool with the ransom of a penny could come true.

But there was no time for dreams or wishes. A second wave climbed from the sea. A towering, frothing monster blocking out the world as it curved up and over them, catching *The Summer Girl* in its curl. Together Rafe and Valentina withstood its force. Gasping and coughing, starved lungs battling to catch a wisp of air, they clung to the wheel and each other in its subsiding wrath.

The storm was a whirling demon, circling, attacking, circling again. The wind howled. It screamed. The bow dipped and reared over rough surf. Wave after wave pounded at them, drenching, choking. There was nothing to be done but stand together, one lending strength to the other, keeping their course.

Their lives lay in the hands of fate and the endurance of *The Summer Girl.*

Time crept. Each minute was timeless. But each was precious, a passage bringing them closer to their goal. For that they persisted.

Valentina grew weary, her arms leaden. Her mind was so dulled to anything but the telescoping effort of survival she was only aware that Rafe had called her name, when he lifted her face in his palm.

"Look, O'Hara!" Rain ran in rivulets down his face. His bandage was crimson, his eye beginning to bruise, but he was laughing. "We made it."

"Eden?" Her heart quickening, eyes straining, at first she saw nothing. Then, gradually, a nebulous form began to take shape. The island lay like a mirage in a circle of gray, the sky and sea the same, with no end and no beginning. Only a blazing line of lights along its shore distinguished the land, drawing them to it.

"Hattie!" Rafe exclaimed. "She knew we'd be coming, riding before the worst of the storm. She knew we would need the lights."

"How could she?" Valentina clung to the helm, with rain and froth from the sea washing about her.

"She has her ways. You'll see."

"I think for now I'll just accept that she does, and be thankful."

"So will I." Recovered, his head clear, taking sole control, he brought the sloop around in a gradual shift of course. "We'll be safe now, O'Hara. The harbor lies on the leeward side of the island. Once there, we can ride out the worst. When it's done, we'll have our time together in Eden."

Valentina made no reply as she stepped aside. Even as *The Summer Girl* made the final turn to the leeward side of the island, she said nothing.

The rage of the storm was still around her. The rage of fear for Rafe still within her. Not even the daze of overwhelming fatigue nor the relative calm of the shielding harbor of Eden could quiet it.

Eleven

Sunlight slanted through the open slats of plantation shutters. Broken by bars of shadow it fell over Valentina's bed. Beyond an open door and a balcony that overlooked the shore, palmettoes rustled in the morning breeze. Their clacking fronds a natural accompaniment for the melodic cadence of the whispering sea.

With the heartbeat of the island sounding music in her ears, with the sun warming her face, she stirred and yawned and purred like a sated kitten. In all her adult life she couldn't remember feeling this contented, this comfortable.

"Eden," she mused as she drowsed. "Where the real world and its troubles cease to exist."

"Oh, they exist, honey girl. Eden just offers respite for a while." The reply was rich and decisive beneath a hint of fond laughter.

Clambering from the covers, leaning against a mound of pillows she'd tossed aside, Valentina blinked and focused her heavy-lidded eyes. And found herself looking sleepily into a beaming, friendly face. "Hattie." Her voice was husky, bluesy, from the length and depth of her slumber. "I'm sorry, I didn't realize you were there."

"No need to be sorry for anything on Eden, honey girl." A vase of the day's fresh flowers in her hand, Hattie Boone moved from the open doorway into the spacious room. Her steps were unhurried and lazy. An impression she projected in all things, until one realized how much she accomplished and how quickly.

"Were you waiting for me to wake?" Casting a glance at the small clock by her bedside, Valentina was appalled at the late hour. "Ten! Good heavens, you must think I'm a laggard to lie in bed so long."

"No such thing." The flowers were placed on a credenza of hand rubbed cherry, replacing yesterday's arrangement that had been removed while Valentina slept. "Eden sets the pace each of us needs. It always has. And what I think is that you have years of rest and peace to catch up. Does my heart good to see you lying there, sleeping away the troubles that were weighing you into the ground."

"But my troubles, great or small, should be no reason to interrupt your schedule, keeping you from your work."

"Keep me from my work." A chuckle erupted from the depths of a massive bosom. A small sphere suspended there by a ribbon of black satin jostled and bumped over great swells, adding music of its own to the day. "You and that black-haired rapscallion are my work. And if you haven't discovered that I love every minute of it, you aren't half so clever as I thought."

It was true, Hattie did love her work. Any visitor to Eden could see that she did, in every move, every gesture. Even so, there was no need to bring disorder to her routine. Putting right the tangle of her clothing, Valentina sighed. "Clever or not, I shouldn't lie abed keeping you from the rest of your day."

"You are the rest of my day," Hattie scolded happily. "And who's to say that whiling away a little time on the balcony is a waste of my time?" Squared shoulders lifted in decisive emphasis. To the trill of the sphere, gaudy earrings of shells and stones swayed against her throat. Lucifer, the tiny monkey that was her ever-present companion, chattered and complained and clung to her blouse to keep his balance on her shoulder.

Every minute was precious to Hattie. And every act she counted an enrichment of her life, be it tallying the twinkles of a star, smelling a flower, or watching the curling waves wash over the shore.

"To be truthful, I was hoping you would sleep longer, mayhap waking with a better appetite after your long fast." Dark, kohl-lined eyes swept over Valentina's body as it made hardly a ripple beneath the sheets of a bed best described as immense. "You could use a pound or two. You have good bones and a good body, but you do look a tad skinny lying there, you know."

Ruefully patting the mattress, Valentina laughed. "Anyone would look small in this bed. Patrick McCallum must think everyone who sleeps here will be the giant I've heard he is."

"You would never be a giant anywhere, in any bed."

"I know." Valentina agreed with her laughter lingering. "Because I'm a 'tad skinny.'"

"A condition I shall do my best to remedy."

"Most immediately, I suspect, with a breakfast cart fit for a queen and enough for a stevedore." Along with everything else, it hadn't taken long for Valentina to see that Hattie Boone was nothing short of amazing in any and all things. Like magic she could produce the most spectacular meals, or the most splendid flower arrangements, or the most constructive wisdom. Yes, she was happiest when she was working, and she made it look easy. And yes, there was nothing she was more adept at than sensing the needs of people. And nothing she liked more than meeting those needs.

One look at Valentina, soaked and shivering from the storm and its ordeal, and every protective and motherly instinct in her amazonian frame leapt to attention. In the week since, she'd never intruded, never presumed, and would have cut her tongue out before she would have questioned. But neither was she ever far away.

"There is a cart waiting on the balcony," Hattie admitted blandly. "But not so much, and not so heavy."

"Just something to tempt the fickle appetite?"

"Fresh fruit and juice. And, mayhap, a scone or two?"

"Two!" Valentina crossed her arms over her breasts and scowled in mock annoyance. "Don't push it."

"Ahh." The heavy earrings swung fiercely now, and Lucifer gave up on his favorite perch. Leaping to the floor, he scampered away. "One wonders how you can resist my special scones. They are..."

"As good for the soul as for the stomach," Valentina finished in unison with her. "Manna from heaven. Patrick's favorite." On her own she continued the list, adding, "If one is good, how much better would two be?"

"Exactly," Hattie boomed, undaunted by hearing her own words given back to her. "Particularly for a wisp of a girl like Valentina O'Hara."

Stretching, with her arms over her head and reaching for the sky, Valentina sighed. "A bit more substantial than a wisp, and not a girl in a long, long while."

"Ha!" A dramatic toss of the sleek, tightly coiffed head, and the sea shells played music of their own. Somewhere in the distant regions of the sprawling house a ringing telephone added another note. The determined caretaker of Eden House ignored it. "Tell that to the Creole who paces the beach like a panther when he's not with you, and watches you like a beam of sunlight could shatter you when he is.

"Hold that thought." A pointing finger emphasized Hattie's directive. "I shall return."

As she disappeared through the open doorway to answer the persistent summons of the telephone, Valentina leaned back against the mountain of pillows she'd declined before. Warmed by the sunlight, soothed by the harmony of the island, she let herself dream of the man who was swiftly becoming the focus of all her dreams.

Rafe.

Beautiful, barbaric, elegant Rafe. Every inch the panther to which Hattie likened him; the dashing Creole she'd named him. Quiet, loyal, as deadly as the panther in the face of danger. Fascinating and intriguing. Everything Valentina O'Hara wanted. Everything that frightened her.

He'd come into her life as only he ever had. Strong, bold, indomitable, challenging her. Questioning not her proficiency, nor Simon's choice, but the quality of compassion. Yet, with doubt still shadowing his brilliant green eyes, he'd held her in the desert, listened to the ranting secrets of sleep, lending his strength, offering silent support. In the end, he'd seen her clearly and judged her fairly. As he'd left her on a bleak and barren mountaintop, it was with a promise.

When he'd come to her, keeping that promise, sensing needs only Simon and her family understood, he'd worked with her, beside her, and for her. Then, showing her the way that life could be, he'd brought her into the home and lives of Jeb and Nicole. And for a time of healing, as she couldn't and hadn't before, he gave her Eden.

From their first step on the island, with Hattie waiting and armed with warmed towels and bolstering drinks, he'd moved into the background. A figure beyond the circle of the daily routine. A smiling, watching presence, never beyond reach. But never an intrusion. Never a part of her life on Eden.

"I've missed you, Rafe Courtenay." The truth she hadn't realized or faced until now rang with the knell of an insistent bell. The lethargy of the past week vanished. Suddenly she couldn't be still, couldn't wait to see him, to tell him what she'd discovered.

Tossing back the covers she bounded to her feet and strode to the closet, peeling away nightclothes as she went. Before the gauzy shirt of lawn drifted to the floor, she was slipping into another of a sturdier fabric, but no less provocative in the absence of a bra. A pair of faded shorts, the tails of the shirt tied at the waist, sandals, a quick comb through the heavy length of her hair, and she was done.

With a mental apology to Hattie for the clutter she was leaving behind, she dashed to the door and the balcony.

"Whoa!" Hattie steadied the smaller woman with one hand and the breakfast cart with the other as they almost collided. "Where are you running off to? Surely you aren't so desperate to avoid my scones."

"Of course I'm not, Hattie." Taking her arm from the supporting grasp, Valentina backed away. "For the first time in a long time, I'm not avoiding anything. Thanks to Jeb, I see beyond the dark side of guilt to the light."

The questions Hattie would never ask were written on her face. Taking both rapier-nailed hands in hers, Valentina explained. "Once there was another man in my life. His name was David, and I loved him very much. When he died, when his life stopped, my life stopped, as well. For reasons I won't go into, to punish myself and keep his memory alive, I never let myself heal. Work and my family became my reasons for existing, and I told myself it was enough.

"Now I know it isn't. Jeb made me see that David wouldn't want it to be. Until now I couldn't face the changes admitting it would bring. I wasn't ready to let David become only a memory.

"I didn't think I ever could." She was speaking rapidly, now, the complexities simplified. "Then there was the storm and Rafe was hurt." Valentina's clasp tightened over Hattie's hand. "If the swell had swamped us, if the blow he took had been even a fraction harder, I could have lost him. In another way, I still might. Maybe it's too late already, yet I have to try, I have to tell him. But first…"

"But first?" Hattie interjected into the rambling discourse that should have made no sense, and yet made perfect sense. A worried frown formed on her face. "What could matter more than simply telling him that you love him?"

Valentina had begun to move away, now she turned back to Hattie. "You know?"

"Of course I know. Isn't loving him and admitting it what this morning has been all about?" Arms like hams folded beneath the shelf of an intimidating bosom. "Even if it weren't, anyone who sees the two of you together would know. Lord love a duck! A total stranger or a fool would know. So what could be more important than sharing this great mutual and public secret with the only one who really matters?"

"Proving it." The ultimate truth faced, Valentina was eager to be away. To begin.

"You have nothing to prove. Rafe doesn't want or need anything but the words."

"I owe him more than that. I have to give him my trust by telling him of my part in David's death. Then, in time, I can only hope he will trust me."

"Valentina, don't complicate matters." Hattie's unique insight warned that her newest charge was still too fragile to risk delays. One misstep, coupled with the voice on the telephone, a voice from her other life, and she could be steeped again in the self-doubt and mistrust she'd brought to Eden. "If Rafe wanted the whole story he could have found out for himself."

"That's the point, Hattie. He could have, but didn't. He respected my wishes and my privacy. I owe him the whole of the truth in return. Yes, he could have found out. A telephone call would have sufficed. But he didn't call. He has said that what I think he must know must come from me."

"Only because he thinks the telling is what you need, not because he wants it. You speak of trust and truth, when it's you who needs to trust that Rafe believes in you, and will believe in you in all things. Past, present, future."

"Hey!" Valentina retraced her steps. Pausing before Hattie, she touched a sculptured brown cheek. "I know you don't understand, but you're worrying when you shouldn't. Time, all I need is time to make it work."

Hattie bit down on her tongue, holding back the warning that time was a luxury she didn't have. That in its stead, all she needed was the faith to trust—as she would be trusted.

"Time and Eden," Valentina explained, taking her proviso one step further. Then she was hurrying away, with Hattie's worried gaze following.

"Wait!" The older woman called out as she started down the steps that would lead to the path to the beach.

Her fingers lightly gripping the balustrade, Valentina halted and turned, an arching brow her query.

Realizing the futility of any argument, abandoning her intended course, Hattie sighed in defeat, saying simply, "You're going the wrong way."

"You said Rafe is walking the beach."

"He was, but not anymore. He's in the library instead."

"The library?"

"The telephone." Hattie halted in a rare loss for words as Valentina blanched beneath her light tan. "The call was for Rafe."

"Patrick?"

Hattie shook her head.

Valentina's light touch became a death grip on the balustrade. Her color descended from pale to ashen. Eyes that should have been dark, sparkling blue were as murky as coal. Tendons at her throat grew taut as she forced a name through rigid lips. "Simon."

Hattie's body heaved in regret. The resultant note of the sphere seemed mournfully discordant. She wanted to cry for the look of devastation that swept away the last of Valentina's elation. "The call was from Simon."

Valentina's hand fell limply to her side. Her tread was heavy as she turned toward the library.

"Too soon the real world," Hattie groused, and would have berated the fates for this importune turn of events. But nothing would change the urgency of the call, or the very real need for Valentina.

As her charge walked stiffly away, the gruff and tender caretaker of Eden watched grim faced. "The real world?" she muttered into the muted music of the island. "If this is what it does to its innocents, then the real world be damned."

The library was deserted. Valentina found Rafe in the salon. A room of grand, unconfined and uncluttered expanses, with columns and great beams where others required walls. A striking blend of eclectic textures and structures. All in a glance from the doorway one could see the tasteful grouping and scattering of dark and pale woods, as well as wicker and cane. Stripes and florals in cottons and silks and simple brocades completed the ambience of what she had come to consider the perfect island house. Perfect in the truest sense of the word, simple, functional, beautiful. Created for a woman who saw with her senses, but never her eyes.

An island haven for Jordana. A gift of reverence and love from Patrick.

Lifting her gaze to the portrait that was, for the sighted, the pièce de résistance, she spoke, drawing Rafe from grim preoccupation. "I wish I could have known her."

His broad back tensing, a scrap of paper crumpling in his hard grasp, he turned slowly to her. "Valentina. I didn't hear you come in."

"I would offer the proverbial coin for the thoughts that had taken you so far away, but I'm not sure it's a bargain I should strike.''

Rafe's head moved once in a negative gesture as his flashing emerald gaze collided with hers. Hoarsely, he said, ''I suppose not.''

An awkward moment passed. Neither wishing to address the telephone call. Neither foolish enough to think it could be avoided. Yet what harm a minute longer?

In measured steps she moved to stand before the portrait. ''Tell me about Jordana.''

Rafe watched her, wondering why this question? Why now? After a moment, crushing the notepaper tighter in his palm, he asked, ''What would you like to know, O'Hara?''

''Oh.'' Valentina's voice was not quite as controlled as she would have wished. ''What she's like. How she copes with a man as dynamic and difficult as Patrick.'' She paused an instant in her rambling query, then began again. ''Most of all, the significance of this painting.''

''You're assuming there is some significance attached to it.''

''Of course. By its mood, by the obvious fact that in a room created for one who can't see, it hangs here. Delicate, exquisite, a remembrance of a cherished moment for a man who can.''

Rafe was struck, again, by Valentina's perception, the almost mystical way she understood the mood of the house, the island. And even Patrick, a man she'd never met.

''You assume correctly.'' Rafe shifted his stance so they were standing side by side. His arm brushed hers beneath the upturned sleeves of his shirt. Desires held in reserve for days, but never cooled, stirred within him. The quickening beat of his heart was uneven as he looked at her, not at the portrait. His voice, when he spoke, was mercifully level. ''This particular painting is more than a flattering likeness. More than a dreamy flight of artistic fantasy. The painting *is* Jordana. It captures the essence of all that she is.

''If you look deeper than with your eyes, you see she's far more than beautiful. She's good and kind and generous, and she's given her heart only once. Only to Patrick. When he's difficult, she simply loves him. As she knows she's loved in return.''

Tearing his stare from Valentina, he looked at the portrait. At Jordana McCallum, all white and golden, caught in a misty sunbeam. *"The Summer Girl*, the incarnation of the dreams of summer. She was modeling for this project when she and Patrick met. He saw her first in a restaurant in Atlanta, and fell into instant lust. It had taken weeks of searching to find the elusive and mysterious Jordana Daniel. On the day his search ended, she was wearing that dress, carrying that hat with its silly wreath of cabbage roses. On that day he discovered for the first time that those marvelous amethyst eyes would never see him. And on that day, he fell irrevocably in love.

"It took the great stubborn Scot a while to admit it, and longer to win the lady. But neither of them regrets what the other is. Patrick would give Jordana her sight, if he could. But for her sake, not his. And as for Jordana, Patrick wouldn't be her great bear of man if he weren't difficult and stubborn at times.''

"The Summer Girl," Valentina observed in a reverent tone. "Portrait of a love story.''

Realizing she'd given a summation more fitting and accurate than any ever made, Rafe added his agreement. "A love story, indeed. And in all the years I've known them, neither has ever faltered. I would wager my life neither ever will.''

Falling silent, he brought to an end a long, complicated story reduced to terms of honor and love. It seemed appropriate and enough.

There was pain and loss in her eyes, but Valentina felt only joy for the woman who had given her heart only once. Who knew lasting love as she never had. As she never would. "You're right, I can see she's beautiful, inside as well as outside. No one deserves happiness more than Jordana.''

"No one?''

Before he could reach out to her, before he could destroy her resolve, Valentina backed away. "I'm sorry, I can't do this.''

Rafe advanced a step, but made no effort to touch her again. "What can't you do, my love?''

"I can't pretend I'm as deserving as Jordana.''

"Deserving?" His brows slanted in a thoughtful frown. "Must one deserve happiness?"

"I suppose not always."

"Then what is it you feel you don't deserve." When she didn't reply, he suggested softly, "Could it be love?" At her sharp gasp, Rafe moved a step closer, his look blazing. "Or have you decided to pretend you aren't in love with me?"

Valentina retreated. There was heartache beneath the bravado in her voice. "I never said that I loved you."

"And I'm not a fool. You aren't the sort of woman who would have made love with me, if you didn't." A wry smile touched his mouth, but not his eyes. "It was love, my love. For real and forever."

"No!" She retreated another step. He followed, his footsteps the slow, gauging tread of a stalking jungle cat.

"No?" A finger raked down her cheek, lingered at the corner of her mouth, before closing into a fist and lifting away. A shattering reminder of the touch of his lips against hers. "Will you lie to me and say that I'm wrong?"

"This isn't about what I feel or what I felt. It's what I am. What I will always be." Grasping his fist in hers, she raised it between them. Opening his unresisting fingers she took the paper from him. Without a glance, as if she could divine its message, she held it there. "This is the definition of my life. If I dare forget, as I almost did today, the telephone will always ring with a summons from Simon. And I will go wherever he needs me. Because I must. I have to."

"The hell you do!"

Valentina wasted no effort in argument. "I thought I could do it. This morning when I woke, it seemed so perfect. So easy to follow Jeb's lead and put it all behind me. And then the call…"

"As easily as that we're back to square one? And you're going to spend the rest of your life atoning for God knows what?"

"It isn't easy. Never easy. Now that you've come into my life—"

"You'll still go."

"—it will only be harder," she finished as if he hadn't interrupted.

"But you'll go." Rafe would be as relentless as she.

"I have no choice."

Raking a hand brutally through his hair, he stared at her. A long, slow perusal. "Then," he began grimly, "perhaps it's time you told me what terrible sin you committed."

"Perhaps it is."

With a gesture, not daring to touch him again, she led him to a cluster of chairs circling a small table. Once seated and committed, she discovered she couldn't look at him. Couldn't risk the contempt she feared would be in the eyes that had once looked at her with desire. Scrubbing her hands over the rough fabric of her shorts, she attempted a rueful smile and rose to pace in restless agitation. "It's funny, I've known for so long that this day was coming. I've gone over what I would say, time and again, until I knew exactly how it should go. And now, I have no idea where to begin."

"Begin with David. He is the first and last of this, isn't he?"

"Of course, he would be."

"David and you."

"Yes. David and I, and a sultry day in August." On that beginning, one painful increment at a time she drew the story from her mind and heart. "We were a team, the best of the unit. David was usually the front man and I stayed in the background." This time the smile she tried for was cold and hard. "You could say he was the decoy, and I the hunter."

"The best shot."

"To my grief."

"And mine, Valentina?" Going to her, staying her with a touch, Rafe ignored her startled recoil. "Will you let a phenomenal ability, perhaps a God-given gift, destroy my life, as well? All because something went wrong on a sultry day in August all those long years ago?"

At her look of shock that he should say this now, he said quietly, "None of this should come as any surprise. I love you. I've told you in every way I knew, except with the declaration. But even then there were the words. I've called you my love. Because it's true. I think it was inevitable from the moment I heard you talking to that great beast of a horse, taming him, soothing him, coaxing the impossible from him and from yourself in return.

"On a barren mountaintop I discovered I needed you. And yes, that need was love. I love a lady of honor and integrity. An amazing lady who rides like the wind and talks to horses. Nothing you've done, nothing you tell me now will change that. Nothing, Irish."

Her heart pounded in her throat like a trip-hammer, her knees threatened to buckle with the weight of grief for what couldn't be. "Nothing?" she asked gravely. "Not even that I killed the one man I've loved before you?"

His expression didn't change so much as a flicker. "Not even that."

"I had a shot!" She was almost desperate to make him understand her fatal error. "For one split second there was an opening. I hesitated. In that second the crazed creature who had taken David hostage fired instead. While I sat there in my safe, protected cubbyhole watching David die, I knew it was as much my fault as if I'd pulled the trigger." She hadn't been able to hold her gaze to his. Suddenly it seemed imperative that she did. "Now, do you see?"

"Better than you realize."

"What does that mean?"

Ignoring her demand, Rafe tried again to assure her. "I didn't need to hear this. I never wanted to hear it."

"But you listened."

"Only because you needed it. Not I."

"That's what Hattie said."

"A wise woman, Hattie. You could do no better than to listen to her."

"You don't understand," Valentina protested. "Neither of you understands."

"I understand better than you think. So does Hattie. You're afraid to love again. Afraid to take a chance on having the life of another man in your hands and your heart. For a little while you fell under the spell of Eden, and this morning you saw hope for a better life. Then the call." A muscle rippled in his cheek, his lips were rigid, his words tight. "A reminder of the real world. And now you're trying to drive me away."

"I'm sorry." The whispered words nearly choked her.

"So am I, my love, and because you need for me to go, I'm going. But only for now, only to leave you to make your plans and prepare for your last mission."

"My last!"

"Yes, your last." Rafe made no other response to her abrupt outcry, and continued in a decisive tone. "When it's done, we have a score to settle. No third party, no baggage from the past. Just you and I, O'Hara."

With her back to the portrait of the woman she admired more than any other, Valentina watched as he spun about to leave. "There's nothing to settle," she called after him. "Nothing more to say."

Halting, Rafe smiled, thoughtfully, indulgently, as if she were a well-loved child. "You're mistaken, my love. There's much to be settled, and much more to be said. Another side of this discussion. Another opinion."

"Another opinion?"

"Exactly." His smile didn't change as he turned away to complete his exit. As he disappeared into the cool shadows of the hall, a single word drifted back to her. "Mine."

The helicopter arrived at dawn. As it descended to the helipad, airfoils setting tree and plant into frenzied cacophony, a very different Valentina was waiting. The gaze she shielded from flying debris was cool and steely. Her moves were exact and confident. She was a professional, returning to the world she knew. One she should never have left. Her night had been spent poring over plans and sketches faxed by Simon. And as the dedicated professional, she'd let nothing intrude in her study.

Her goodbyes to Hattie had been made at the breakfast the caretaker had insisted on making for her. She knew she was more than honest when she'd admitted she would miss that handsome, smiling face.

The lie she told herself was that she would not miss Rafe. That she had not in the long night. That it didn't hurt when he hadn't come to say goodbye.

Her meager luggage was loaded. The pilot of the helicopter waited and watched expectantly. Time had already been lost, and was of the essence, but still she loitered. Waited. Watched. Hoped.

Nothing. No one.

"Miss O'Hara, ma'am." Though he seemed oddly uncertain, the pilot called over the roar of engines, "We have to go."

"I know," she responded without moving. "Just give me a minute. I'm going to miss this place and the people."

"Even me, O'Hara?" Rafe stepped through the fog of dust and sand.

"Rafe!" Only a resolve of iron kept her from throwing herself into his arms. From kissing his beloved mouth. "You came to say goodbye."

"Not just yet." He tossed a bag into the open door of the chopper. "I'm going with you."

"You're what? Why?" Then, realizing that he looked tired, she exclaimed, "You look exhausted. Is your head bothering you? Have you slept?"

"My head's fine, healing right on schedule. As for the rest of your barrage of questions, we'll have plenty of time to discuss them later." Taking her arm, he led her to the chopper. A second after he joined her on board, he tapped the pilot's helmet. "Any time you're ready, Tommy."

"Yes, sir."

In a surge of engines and a bluster of sand the helicopter lifted to the sky. For a time, conversation was impossible. Her questions would have to wait. Amid the clamor, as they climbed, Valentina looked down, saying a private farewell to Eden, mourning for the end of the dream she'd only dare to dream by its shore.

"Wrong again, O'Hara." As the engines quieted, Rafe took her hand in his.

She looked from his face to their joined hands and back. "How can I be wrong when I've said nothing? Playing the clairvoyant again? Reading my mind?"

"No need."

"I haven't said anything, and you aren't reading my mind, yet you know I'm wrong?"

"You got it!"

"Yeah?"

"Yeah! You're thinking this is the end." With his thumb he stroked the back of her hand. "When it's really only the beginning."

"Rafe..."

"Shh." He silenced her with a kiss. A fleeting brush of his lips that stole thought and reason away.

"What about David?" She struggled back on track.

"What about him?" Before she could answer, he growled, "Forget I said that. Let's not talk about David. Look, sweetheart, you're right, I'm tired and I didn't sleep last night. If you don't mind, I think I'll catch a nap."

Sliding down in his seat, he slipped on a cap and tipped the brim over his face. With his fingers twined through hers, and his hand heavy on her lap, he slept, or pretended to sleep.

Valentina's mind was in turmoil, her heart in a quandary. Why was Rafe here? What did it mean? Why, even in sleep, did he grip her hand as if he would never let her go?

Questions beat at her with the chop-chop rhythm of the helicopter. Unsettling, frightening questions with no answers.

Questions that opened door to dreams she'd put aside.

"No," she muttered and slammed it shut again. The Black Watch was her life and her future. Not Rafe.

For the remainder of the flight, with only the chill of her hand warmed by his, she stared with dry and melancholy eyes at the distant landscape.

Twelve

"Careful! Watch that telephone line."

Valentina was only vaguely aware of Simon's stern caution. In the depth of her concentration she'd blanked out the crew hovering in the adjoining hotel room. Given her choice she would have had the connecting doors closed, the lights out. If there had been functioning air-conditioning, it would be turned low, the circulating fan off. Then she would be completely isolated, without a sound, in a frigid vacuum. Not even a current of arctic air would disturb her riveting study of the room a story lower and an angling block away. The room where Bryson Lewis, electronic wizard, bankrupt millionaire, suspected embezzler and murderer, held his ex-wife hostage.

All Valentina's choices were impossible. Her post was a flop house. Any days of opulence and prosperity it ever boasted were long gone and long forgotten. The only amenities accorded its current tenants, the recently evacuated transients, were toilets, unheated water, soiled mattresses for sleeping off hangovers from whatever drug or drink imbibed, and electricity.

In her first reconnoitering inspection on arrival, she'd seen that Lewis had chosen well in his bastion of revenge. In time, his skewed genius and thorough planning grew increasingly evident at every turn. In a dying city in the mid-South, where industry absconded like fabled rats scrambling from a sinking ship, he'd commandeered the most isolated complex of all. The one he knew best. His own.

Its derelict buildings, all that remained of his once sprawling empire, marched in tumbledown rows. Blanketing vines of twisting and coiling kudzu, creeping plague of the fallow South, drifted from them in ghostly shreds. Of the decaying facilities he'd chosen the main office. A one-story, ground-hugging structure that defied invasive approach. Had it not, the surrounding grounds were guarded by sophisticated electronic surveillance. For fail-safe measures, there were mines and traps beyond comprehension of the sane mind.

In his descent into mad-dog hatred of the world and particularly his wife, Lewis had planned well and prepared thoroughly for his grand finale.

The first plan of attack by the local chief of police had been straightforward and logical: interrupt the source of electricity. Wait him out and, under a cover of darkness, with specially trained dogs and a bomb squad, infiltrate his fortification.

Lewis was a step ahead, promising Betty Lewis would die as the first light went out. In that precedent, every option was met with the same promise.

The bottom line was that no one expected that either Lewis would survive. It was clearly never Bryson Lewis's intent that they should.

A grave and desperate situation even more grave and desperate than anyone had realized. With every avenue blocked, only one option remained. A call went out. Simon responded.

The situation became the sole jurisdiction of The Black Watch.

A team was chosen, possibilities and probabilities weighed, choices were made. Their last recourse confronted, an agent, the only agent capable of what would be asked, was summoned.

The interval of theorizing ended. It was time to act. Drifters and panhandlers were removed from this structural detritus. Phone lines were set up, communication established with

Lewis. Less than twenty-four hours after Simon's initial call, Valentina, a specter in black, crouched by a window, alone in a room little better than a pigsty, waiting for a madman to show himself.

When he did, if he did, her opportunity for a clean shot would be slim to none. From an impossible distance, the targeted window was only partially visible through a vine covered fence and the rubble of other buildings. One desperate chance was all she would have, and Valentina knew Betty Lewis's life hinged on that chance.

She needed a clue, an edge, something to anticipate and lead the man.

"But what?" The words were a breath, a sigh. A minor stirring in the mounting heat of Indian summer that so often followed an early autumn in the South. Her shirt had long been plastered to her body. Her hair clung damply to her neck and throat. Sweat burned her eyes, often blurring her vision. But she never looked away. Never forgot the hostage woman.

Stripped of any gewgaws to glint in the light, she wore no watch. In the passing of the day, though she had only a vague idea of the hour, judging it solely by the angle of the sun, a silent clock ticked in her head. She could feel it, time was running out.

Dear heaven! She needed a clue. Just one.

"Here, sweetheart, drink this."

"What?" The gentle intrusion was no match for the intensity of her escalating concern.

A cool glass touched her heated cheek as Rafe knelt beside her. "It isn't much. Only tap water, but maybe a little better than a canteen baked by the sun on an Arizona mountaintop."

Arizona.

Valentina's mind was suddenly scrambling to catch a niggling, fading idea.

With another light touch at her cheek, Rafe urged again, "Drink. Please. I promise I won't make a habit of diverting your attention, but you've been here for hours. Soon you'll be cramping from dehydration."

Valentina stared straight ahead, eyes narrowed, her mind buzzing from the effort to make a connection.

ArizonaArizonaArizona.

The chanting litany seared her brain, but her most vivid impression was the telltale slide of a rattler's scales over barren red rock.

Her hands clenched, and her teeth. Tendons in her throat pulled tight. What was it she should remember?

The first stirrings of a cramp began deep in tense muscles. A reminder that Rafe was there by her side.

"Thanks, you're right." She took the glass from him, grateful that he made no small talk. That he understood she mustn't be distracted. A fast gulp, a swipe of her arm across her forehead, another sip and she had enough to suffice.

Rafe took the half-filled glass from her, but did not return to the next room where Simon and a crew plotted and planned, anticipating any circumstance. Valentina seemed so small and drawn, too fragile for the task she'd been given. The burden of two lives was too much for anyone to bear alone. He would have taken a share of it from her, damning those responsible, but he knew she wouldn't allow it. So he did what little he could, lingering, hoping she would gather added strength from his mute support.

Her attention remained fixed on the window, yet, in another part of her mind, Valentina was keenly conscious of him. With each breath his clean, masculine scent filled her lungs, a merciful relief from the stale odors left by the last tenant. Though she made no acknowledgment she became increasingly aware that his voice still echoed in her mind. Something only her subconscious had perceived in her focused intensity.

Her thoughts still ranging, searching, in an absent motion she reached out to stroke the polished stock of her rifle. Taking it as his cue to leave, certain he would get her to drink nothing more, Rafe started to rise.

Her fingers closed roughly over his wrist. "Stay."

When he glanced at her, he found she hadn't turned from her study of the office where Betty Lewis could very well be suffering through her last hours. "Of course," he assured her. "I'll be here for as long as you wish."

The beginning of a frown lined her face, her hold on his wrist grew harder. "Something you said…"

Rafe could almost feel her struggle as she tried to make some connection. "Something I said? When?"

"Now." With a grimace she qualified, "But not exactly."

Rafe was on track immediately, his mind working in tandem with hers. As no stranger to elusive ideas, he knew the frustration of perceptions buried too deeply to surface. Mentally retracing his steps, replaying his conversation in his own mind, he began to walk her through it one phrase at a time. "I asked you to drink."

Releasing him, with her fingertips she massaged the painful muscles at her temples. Her eyes closed briefly; her head tilted from side to side. "No."

"It isn't much but..." Rafe continued his recounting.

"Better than a canteen on an Arizona mountaintop!" She finished for him and was clearly eager that he go on.

"I asked you to drink again."

This time her head only jerked once in negative response.

"I promise not to make a habit..."

"Habit!" She turned to him then, looked at him for the first time in hours. There was incredible fatigue in her face, but her eyes were alive with hope. "That's it. I'd only just arrived the last time Simon spoke to Lewis on the telephone. I caught a glimpse of him at the window, but I was setting up." Then angrily, "It didn't register."

She paused for breath, but Rafe said nothing. He wanted to take her in his arms, to hold her, and keep her, sparing her what was coming. But he kept his own counsel, knowing how fragile a half-remembered nuance could be. How easily it could be lost.

"It was there all along and I didn't see it." Valentina was whispering to herself, letting the idea grow as it would. "Erratic, unstable, compulsive. He paces when he talks on the telephone. A creature of ingrained habits. That's it! That's the key. Lewis is like Brown."

"Ten puffs," Rafe murmured, his voice hoarse with emotion, quoting her from a memory forever branded in his mind. "Not nine, not eleven. Ten." Leaving the remainder unspoken, he addressed the present. "You're thinking Lewis will keep strongly to habit under pressure. So many paces in each direction while he talks on the phone."

"If we're lucky."

"Let's say we are. If that's the case, each pass by the window could be timed."

"Each pass by the part of the window I can see," she corrected.

"Yes, dammit! Part of the window." And so long as Lewis didn't suspect her presence, her purpose, he thought. The enormity of what she'd been asked to do, the impossibility of what was expected of her infuriated him. But his fury was a luxury Valentina couldn't afford. It was his help, not his anger, she needed. "At best, even if he paces slowly, that would give you...how many seconds?"

"I don't know." Then honestly, "Not enough."

"You have to anticipate. Lead him."

"That's right."

"If you're wrong, and you miss..."

"Betty Lewis is as good as dead." Her face was grim, but she was the cool professional once more. The excitement of discovery calming, she had a job to do. A life to save.

"But if you don't try..."

"She'll die." Valentina didn't look at him again as she took up her weapon.

"That doesn't make it any easier, does it?"

"Not for me, and not for her two little girls." She was staring down at the window, engrossed again in the plight of a young mother, when she said in a level monotone, "I'm ready. Would you ask Simon to make the call? Explain that I need as long as he can give me to establish a pattern—if there is one. Tell him—" she hesitated, her tongue moving over dry, pale lips "— tell him, let's make this count. I have a gut feeling time's not on our side."

Rafe was standing now, looking down at her. "Anything else?"

"Nothing," she answered shortly, anxious that he go to Simon, to set into motion this last-ditch plan. A minute sped by, then she heard his footsteps crossing the bare floor. As a board by the door that always creaked protested his passage she called to him. "Rafe."

The silence of total stillness told her he had stopped. Perhaps that he had turned back, that he waited. Her throat was suddenly clogged with emotion she couldn't afford. Not now.

"Never mind," she managed at last. The board creaked again. There was the murmur of guarded voices before she whispered, "Thanks."

Simon's response seemed to take an eternity. Finally she heard him saying, "Lewis, this is Simon McKinzie."

She heard no more, but it was enough. His voice became a gruff drone fading into the background. Words she heard, but made no effort to distinguish. What Simon said was of little consequence. All that mattered was time. Time to seek out a pattern. To find its rhythm.

"All right, Bryson Lewis," she muttered, her cheek against the stock of the rifle. "Do your thing," she coaxed. "Come to the window. Yes. Yes! That's it! Pace." Beginning her count, she tracked Lewis's brief passages by the sliver of window visible to her. Hardly daring to breathe, she counted, tracked, prayed. Counted, tracked, prayed. Then...

"Gotcha!"

She had the cadence. With instincts that set her apart, without thinking or understanding how, she knew the milliseconds of lead time, the trajectory. But not the margin for human whim.

Her finger squeezed gently on the trigger. "Don't," she whispered hoarsely, haltingly. "Don't...break...habit... Now!"

She never heard the blast of the powerful rifle nor the shattering of glass. She never saw her target. Yet she knew the bullet had gone home, that Bryson Lewis would never harm anyone again. As she laid the rifle aside, she knew, as well, that she would never fire it again.

When she turned from the window, she found Rafe standing in the open doorway. Hair disheveled, face ashen. His eyes like green, fathomless pools, watching her with their worried gaze.

"It's over, Rafe."

"Thank God," he muttered hoarsely. "And you."

"You were right," she said, neither noting nor comprehending his tribute. "This was the last time."

Drawing a long, hard breath, Rafe found he could only nod. Oblivious of the commotion of Simon's men deploying to complete the rescue, he said at last, "I suppose you have some thinking to do."

"When it's truly over, I will. After Lewis's traps and gizmos have been defanged. Once I know for sure she's safe." The list dragged on. "After I'm debriefed."

"But you're all right, for now?"

"As all right as one can be when…"

"When a life has been saved," Rafe interrupted determinedly.

"And one taken. I can't forget that part."

"No one expects you to."

"But I'm supposed to deal with it."

"Can you?"

"Yeah." Her expression was grave, filled with sorrow. But there was strength in her voice. "This time I can."

He wanted to go to her, wrap himself around her, but he held himself aloof. She was vulnerable now, and the choices she made must be hers. Not his. "You'll be busy for some time."

Valentina nodded. "With the investigation. The reports. With the counseling Simon requires."

All she could cope with for a while. He would be excess baggage, a hindrance and a distraction. There was nothing more he could do here. Nothing he could do for her. Not yet. He made a sudden decision. "Then I'll be on my way."

Surprise flickered in her face. "Where will you go?"

Rafe managed a grim smile. "Not far. If you really want to find me, it shouldn't be too hard." He turned to go, then stepped back around. "I left some papers for you with Simon. Information I spent most of last night gathering." Was it only last night he'd contacted Patrick, and between them called in every favor ever owed them, incurring a few along the way? With every one of them worth it. "I think you'll find the report interesting reading."

"What papers? What report?"

She was nearing the end of her stamina. He could see it in her stance, hear it in her voice. "Nothing urgent," he assured her. "Get some rest. Do what Simon requires. When you have a moment and the inclination, read them."

"Then what?"

"That, my love, I leave to you." Standing as he was, he looked at her for a long while, his gaze touching her, caressing. "Be well, Irish." His voice was deep, thoughtful. "Be happy."

He left her then, standing in the middle of the barren room of a deserted hotel, more lost and alone than she'd ever been.

The island hadn't changed. It came as a shock to her that it hadn't. In the two weeks since she'd visited with Betty Lewis and her children, feeling the love between them, seeing the mending and sharing it, Valentina felt as if the whole world had altered. It had become, for her, a new world. One Rafe had given her.

"How long?" She glanced over her shoulder at Jeb Tanner.

"Five minutes less than the last time you asked." He grinned at her from his place at the wheel of the small sloop he called *Tanner's Lady*, for Nicole. "That makes it ten total."

"Ten." In ten minutes she would be in Rafe's arms.

Jeb chuckled. "Nine minutes too long?"

"Nine and a half."

"You know this is what you want? You're sure now?"

"I'm sure." A freshening breeze teased at the bill of the cap she wore. Catching at it, she tugged it lower, shielding her face from the sun. "Thanks to you."

"Hey, I just told the truth. But if it helped, I'm glad. Nicole sends her love and good wishes, by the way."

"How is she?"

"A little queasy." Jeb beamed. "The doctor assures us it will pass."

"Does it scare you?"

"Having a baby?" He grew sober. "Scares the hell out of me." Then he laughed. "I'm so damn proud I need a hat two sizes bigger."

"Any regrets?"

"Only that it took so long to reach this point."

"Any doubts?"

"About the choices I've made? About my life as it is? Not one." From his vantage, he watched her as she turned in profile to gaze at Eden, lying like an emerald in a sea of silver-capped turquoise. "It will be the same for you one day. I promise."

Valentina kept her gaze on Eden. "I hope so."

They were close. So close she could distinguish the small cabana on the strip of gleaming sand. A shanty, really, of posts and thatch. A respite from the sun for beachcombers and surf fishing. A shelter for making love after a lazy day of salt and sand.

"Coming here is a good beginning." Pausing, Jeb added gently, "He loves you, Valentina."

"I know."

"He believes in you. The report was for you, not for himself."

The report! The amazing, overwhelming body of evidence suggesting more than strongly, if not proving conclusively, that only a miracle could have saved David Flynn. Revealing facts and circumstance that, in her guilt, Valentina had pushed to the back of her mind. Though there would always be that painful margin of doubt, a burden as weighty as the planet had been lifted from her heart.

Gathering such a body of information, sifting through it, analyzing and organizing it into the crisply worded report was an astounding achievement. "I'll never understand how he accomplished what he did in the length of time he had, Jeb."

"Don't try to understand. Just accept that he did. Just understand why." Jeb saw no reason to expound on the exorbitant cost nor the number of teams of experts who worked through the night unearthing every file and every scrap of film of that day. The processes used to study and analyze what they'd found were too intricate and complicated to try. With a dismissing grin, he drawled, "Modern technology! Ain't it grand."

Valentina wouldn't be sidetracked so easily. "If the report hadn't been favorable, would I have seen it?"

Jeb grew solemn, giving her query the consideration it merited. "Yes." He watched as her body stiffened. "You would have seen it."

"Then what?"

"If you're asking would Rafe had gone away? No, Valentina. Not in a million years, if fate would give him that long. Not unless you sent him away.''

"He left me before. Once Betty Lewis was safe.''

"He gave you space and the time you needed.''

"Is this a test, making me come to him?''

"A choice. Not a test.'' A slight adjustment of course, and the sloop began the turn that would lead to the dock on the leeward side of the island. "A question for you, my dear.''

"All right.'' She turned to him then, waiting.

"If the report had been different, if it hadn't been favorable, would you have come to him? Would you be standing on the deck of *Tanner's Lady* as you are today?''

Her fingers gripping the coaming, she looked again to the island. The small seaside garden that was Jordana's favorite was briefly visible. Within its iron fence a young girl and a younger boy kept their eternal watch over it. Children of a century before, lost to the sea. A memory captured in bronze.

As David was a memory. The sweet memory he should be. If he could see her now, if he was there in the billowing, ever-changing clouds, he would be smiling down at her. She was certain of it.

"And I would be here.'' She spoke the thought aloud. To Jeb. To herself. "Rafe has given me back my life. But without him to share it, what would any of it be?''

Then, soundlessly, to the wind, to her first love, she whispered, "I love him, David.''

Closing her eyes against the ache of loss, she said goodbye.

Then *Tanner's Lady* was nudging the dock, and strong arms were reaching for her. Enfolding her. The voice she loved above all else murmured thickly, "Welcome home, Irish.''

"We should be thinking about getting up and getting dressed.''

"Why?'' Rafe teased and leaned over her to kiss her bare breast and then her laughing lips. "I like you much better lying in bed and undressed.''

"Ahh, that being the case, you shouldn't have planned this splendid ceremony and its great surprise.'' With a subtle shift of her body against his, Valentina paid him back in kind. "The bride and groom can hardly while away the morning in bed when guests will be arriving at any second.''

"We can't?''

"It doesn't seem quite proper. Traditionally, the groom shouldn't even see the bride before the ceremony.''

Rafe chuckled as he looked down at her, naked and tousled and desirable. "Then you intend to be a very proper, very traditional bride?''

"Hardly. It's a little late for proper and traditional, wouldn't you say?'' Valentina laughed, too, the smoky, sexy laugh he loved. Then almost lost the thought as his clever mouth explored the new and ever sweeter paths his gaze had taken. Catching handfuls of his hair, she dragged his mouth back to hers. "We shouldn't,'' she protested between yearning kisses. "We really shouldn't.''

"No?''

"No.'' Even in denial, her eyes sparkled in delight.

Her days on Eden, then at her lodge, had been filled with wonder and passion, magnified by the excitement and great mystery surrounding the planned festivities. Her family would be coming from scattered parts of the world: her parents from their part of the bay, Patience and Matthew from their ranch in Arizona, Tynan from Montana, Kieran from Egypt, and Devlin from wherever the message found him.

The McCallums were coming from Sedona, Jeb and Nicole from Charleston, and Simon from his mountain retreat. With him would be Mitch and Katherine Ryan, and Hunter and Raven Slade.

The party grew: the mystery deepened.

Even Hattie had to agree to a rare sojourn from her beloved Eden to attend the preparations and work her culinary magic. And magic it seemed, indeed.

All very intriguing. All very exciting. But nothing to compare with waking up each morning with Rafe at her side. With the memory of his love like a dream come true.

"The morning's young yet.'' Rafe kissed her throat and nibbled at her ear. "I couldn't change your mind?'' Dancing fingertips traced the line of her throat, the crest of her breast, and came to rest on the flat plane of her belly. "Or prove how wrong you are?''

"Well." Sighing in mock uncertainty, she shifted again, not so subtly. Her palms skimmed over his bare chest, her nails curling into the thick pelt swirling in a narrowing spiral to the sheet that barely covered his hips. "You could try."

"I could, but on second thought, you're right." Levering away from her, he rolled to the edge of the bed. "We shouldn't."

"Rafe Courtenay, you devil!" Catching at his arm as he pretended to rise, she drew him back. "If you know what's good for you, you'll stay right here, in this bed, and finish what you started."

"I will?" His smile was wicked as he returned to her.

"Indeed. Considering."

"Ahh, I see. Considering." A brow tilted over green, blazing eyes. "That you want me madly, I suppose."

"How did you know?"

"Lucky guess."

The teasing suddenly gone from her, she looked into his searing gaze. "You don't need to guess. You never have to guess."

In a whirl of tousled sheets, he tumbled with her. "Show me." Lifting her over him, he eased her down, letting her take him, all of him. "Finish what I started." His voice was rough with desire only she could answer. An ache only she could ease. "Make love to me, Irish."

"Yes and yes and yes." Leaning over him, she let the sway of her body and the brushing caress of her hair tease him. And then her lips, the tips of her breasts. In dappled morning light she was glorious. "My love, Mr. Courtenay, and my pleasure."

"Wrong again." He drew her down to him as quickening shudders began to build within him. In whispers against her trembling lips, as he took her deeper into ecstasy that found its mate in him, he promised, "Ours, Mrs. Courtenay. Always and forever ours."

"Always." Valentina sank into his embrace, sated, content, happier than she ever thought she could be. "And forever."

Beyond mullioned windows, a blue heron stalked the edge of the lawn. The morning sun shone down on a world in full blaze of autumn, while the tidewater of the Chesapeake lapped in its everlasting cadence at the shore. From the kitchen of the lodge, Hattie's voice lifted in song as she worked, readying for this special day.

A day to celebrate.

Thirteen

She stood on the shore, the sound of the tide surrounding her, supplanting the laughter of departed family and friends. Reaching out, she stroked the smooth folds of a gown of bronze. "She's beautiful. Much more than I ever dreamed she could be. A surprise worth all the mystery and intrigue, and my banishment from the shore since we came from Eden.

"I won't ask how you managed all of this." In an encompassing circle, Valentina included the sculpture, newly set stepping stones, and plantings that created the small seaside garden. Caressing Rafe's cheek, she smiled. "I've discovered you can accomplish anything you set your mind to, in a heartbeat and a blink of an eye."

Keeping her hand briefly in his, he turned his mouth into her palm. A kiss as tender as the look in his eyes. "She could be you," he said thoughtfully. "The moment I saw her at the gallery, though Hunter had never met you or even seen you, I knew she was you.

"Serendipity or fate, expressed in an artist's vision?" There was gentle irony in the curve of his smile. "I've always been the emphatic realist, but I've no explanation for her...except that she was meant to be, and that one day she would come here."

Freedom, Hunter Slade's original bronze of a lovely woman with a sea hawk lifting from her hands, had, indeed, found the perfect place. It seemed right that she be there by the bay, that she stood facing the sea, keeping her watch.

"Someone to welcome us each time we come home," Rafe commented quietly.

"Someone to welcome us each time we return to the lodge," Valentina corrected. Stepping into his embrace, she stood on tiptoe to kiss him. "Wherever we go, whatever we do, whatever life brings to us, I'm home, here in your arms."

"Irish." He drew her close, held her tighter. "I love you."

"I know." Turning in his embrace, she nestled back against his hard, broad chest. Her arms folded over his at her waist. "If I didn't, all I would need to do is look at her. The symbol of all you've given me."

"Freedom?"

"Freedom," she looked to the bronze sea hawk, lifting from a bronze hand. "But first courage. The courage to let David go. To live again." Turning in the shelter of his arms, she lifted her lips to his kiss, murmuring softly as her mouth opened to his, "To love again."

Fate or serendipity? Who would ever know?

All that really mattered was that out of tragedy had come fulfillment, and Valentina had come full circle. She had come home.

Where her dreams would be dreams of a green eyed panther from the bayous.

Where whispers in the dark would be whispers of love.

*   *   *   *   *

Don't miss the next story about
THE BLACK WATCH,
*JOURNEY'S END coming to you in early 1998 only in
Silhouette Desire!*

Bestselling author

JOAN JOHNSTON

continues her wildly popular miniseries with an
all-new, longer-length novel

The Virgin Groom

HAWK'S WAY

One minute, Mac Macready was a living legend in
Texas—every kid's idol, every man's envy, every
woman's fantasy. The next, his fiancée dumped him,
his career was hanging in the balance and his future
was looking mighty uncertain. Then there was the
matter of his scandalous secret, which didn't stand a
chance of staying a secret. So would he succumb to
Jewel Whitelaw's shocking proposal—or take cold
showers for the rest of the long, hot summer...?

Available August 1997
wherever Silhouette books are sold.

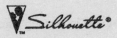

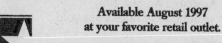

New York Times bestselling author

LINDA LAEL MILLER

Two separate worlds, denied by destiny.

THERE AND NOW

Elizabeth McCartney returns to her centuries-old family home
in search of refuge—never dreaming escape would lie over a
threshold. She is taken back one hundred years into the past and
into the bedroom of the very handsome Dr. Jonathan Fortner,
who demands an explanation from his T-shirt-clad "guest."

But Elizabeth has no *reasonable* explanation to offer.

Available in July 1997 at your favorite retail outlet.

MIRA The brightest star in women's fiction

Coming this July...

Fast paced, dramatic, compelling... and most of all, passionate!

For the residents of Grand Springs, Colorado, the storm-induced blackout was just the beginning. Suddenly the mayor was dead, a bride was missing, a baby needed a home and a handsome stranger needed his memory. And on top of everything, twelve couples were about to find each other and embark on a once-in-a-lifetime love. No wonder they said it was 36 Hours that changed *everything!*

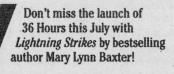

Don't miss the launch of 36 Hours this July with *Lightning Strikes* by bestselling author Mary Lynn Baxter!

Win a framed print of the entire 36 Hours artwork! See details in book.

Available at your favorite retail outlet.

36IBC-R

COMING NEXT MONTH

#1087 NOBODY'S PRINCESS—Jennifer Greene

Alex Brennan, August's *Man of the Month,* was a white knight looking for a fair maiden to love. Regan Stuart was a beauty who needed someone to awaken her sleeping desires…and Alex was more than willing to rescue this damsel in distress.

#1088 TEXAS GLORY—Joan Elliott Pickart

Family Men

Posing as sexy Bram Bishop's wife was the closest to marriage headstrong Glory Carson ever wanted to come. But it didn't take much acting to pretend that the most wanted bachelor in Texas was the prince of her dreams.

#1089 ANYBODY'S DAD— Amy Fetzer

Mother-to-be Tessa Lightfoot's solo baby parenting plans didn't include Chase Madison, the unsuspecting sperm bank daddy. But if Tessa didn't keep him out of her life, she didn't know how much longer she could keep him out of her bed.

#1090 A LITTLE TEXAS TWO-STEP—Peggy Moreland

Trouble in Texas

Leighanna Farrow wanted a home, a family and a man who believed in happily-ever-after. Hank Braden wanted Leighanna. Now, the sexiest, most confirmed bachelor in Temptation, Texas, was about to learn what this marriage business was all about.…

#1091 THE HONEYMOON HOUSE—Patty Salier

For better or worse, Danielle Ford had to share close quarters with her brazenly male colleague, Paul Richards. And his sizzling overtures were driving her to dream of her own honeymoon house.

#1092 UNEXPECTED FATHER—Kelly Jamison

Jordan McClennon was used to getting what he wanted, and he wanted former flame Hannah Brewster and the little boy he thought was their son. But when the truth came out, would it change how he felt about this ready-made family?